THE BARONS OF BEHAVIOUR

THE BARONS
OF
BEHAVIOUR

TOM PURDOM

LONDON : DENNIS DOBSON

Copyright © 1972 by Tom Purdom

First published in Great Britain in 1977
by Dobson Books Ltd, 80 Kensington Church Street,
London W8 4BZ

*Printed in Great Britain by
Clarke, Doble & Brendon Ltd,
Plymouth and London*

ISBN 0 234 77543 2

I

Nicholson stopped walking on the outskirts of the development some real estate developer's advertising department had decided to call Greenplace. He took the drug injector out of his shirt pocket and lowered himself into the wheelchair. For a moment the injector trembled above the lower half of his biceps.

He twisted around in the chair and looked up at the big man standing behind him, the sec he had hired to push him around while he was drugged. "We may get into a fight," he said. "Will you give me a hand if I have to fight?"

The sec stared down at him. He looked like a man who would enjoy tossing people around. He was stiff and formal, and he looked at the world around him with the wooden contempt of a man who hated a society that made such trivial use of muscles. Secs had been the lowest class of unskilled labor ever since the invention of the voicetyper had made the old trade of stenographer-typist obsolete. Usually a sec was just a living status symbol, a set of muscles hired to carry some professional man's files and dictating equipment.

"I don't get paid to fight," the sec said. "You didn't ask for a bodyguard."

"How much would you charge if I paid you extra?"

"I don't get paid to fight."

Nicholson turned around in the chair. He stared at the lawns and houses across the street with the wry, lopsided smile that was so much a part of his personality four of his five daughters had imitated it before they were three. The Lone Knight confronted the fortress of the enemy. The daring and resourceful fighter for right and freedom reconnoitered the battleground with his keen, experienced eye and wished his damned hands would stop shaking.

The tube glued to the middle finger of his left hand was a nonlethal personal defense weapon called a scrambler—a finger-length generator that fired a tight beam of sound and light in a pattern designed to disrupt the human nervous system. He had a pair of bombs loaded with high pressure psycho-active gas in his left shirt pocket, and he had installed a sound generator and an odor generator in the bottom of the wheelchair. He didn't know what the two generators could do for him if he got into trouble, but they had been the only other portable weapons he could think of that looked like he might be able to use them while he was drugged. He had selected the strongest psychic energizer on the market—a combination of modified enzymes that increased the powers of observation and the rate and quality of thought by a factor between three and seven—and the drug had one bad side effect. His coordination would be completely disrupted as soon as the drug started working on his metabolism. He would be a helpless blob of flesh for the next four hours.

He held the injector above his biceps again. His hand trembled again. He shook his head and pressed the release. Two cc's of red liquid shot into his flesh. The sec stiffened and he put the injector back in his pocket.

Children ran and yelled in the yards across the street. Lawn mowers hummed across the grass while their owners watched them with sleepy eyes. It was a sunny Saturday afternoon in June and he was sitting in the shade of the last apartment tower for nearly a mile. Greenplace had been built in the early 1970's, and it was a typical example of the developments that had been built in that era. Every block had less than fifteen houses. Every house had its own lawn and back yard.

His heart started pounding. He glanced at his chest and shook his head. All over his body the chemistry of fear was mingling with the disturbing chemistry of the drug. This was only the second time he had entered the Fifth Congressional District. This time the Boyd organization knew he was coming.

His head rolled to one side. He scanned the clouds and the blue sky and estimated the wind velocity and the kind of weather they were having in Nigeria—the country in which his oldest daughter was spending the second semester of the fourth grade. His right hand suddenly appeared between his eyes and the clouds. He tried to return it to the arm of the chair and slapped his thigh hard enough to sting.

He tried to lower his hand and look at Greenplace and found himself looking at the apartment tower instead. He noted the number of floors and the number of windows per floor and developed a highly original theory about the effects of high-rise apartment living, combined with current toilet training procedures, on the Oedipus complex of classic Freudian psychology. He jerked his head away from the tower and his drug-accelerated brain composed a witty paragraph about the theory for his popular column in *Current Psychology* before the last window slid out of his field of vision.

"Let's ... g ... g ... goooo. ..."

The sec pushed him forward. The landscape swung past his swaying head. He heard the wheels of the chair rumble on the street and he calculated how much heat they were generating and formulated two contradictory hypotheses about what the motion of all the wheeled vehicles on Earth was doing to the annual temperature and rainfall of the northeastern United States.

The sec rolled him off the street onto the sidewalk. Two boys mounted on electric rhinos were engaging in a duel with stunner swords on the first lawn. A heavy man in dirty shorts and an unbuttoned shirt looked away from the duel and glanced at the wheelchair. The man's eyes narrowed. His face hardened and he stuck a cigar butt in his mouth.

Nicholson's head rolled again. People stared at him from the other side of the street. Every eye on the block over twelve years old was focused on him. They had known what he was doing as soon as they had seen him coming. Psych technicians were manipulating them all the time but they still resented it. Very few or-

7

ganizations did their psych surveys this openly any-more. A big organization like Boyd's could study the voters without filling a psychologist with a drug and sending him out in a wheelchair.

Turbines whined in his ear. "Cop," the sec grunted.

An air cushion police car swung past his bobbing head. Two policemen and a dog stared at him from the front seat.

The policemen slid out of his vision. For a moment he and the fat man with the cigar eyed each other. The boys had stopped jousting and the man was stand-ing with his legs spread and his arms folded on his chest in front of the exact center of his house. There was a comical resemblance between the human figure and the front of the house. They were both extremely broad for their height. The fat man had a fat house. . . .

"Just a minute, mister. Hold on."

Fear erased everything but the policemen from his nervous system. Every detail of their appearance regis-tered on his sensitized consciousness and he formu-lated three hypothetical models of their personality structure and started working out a test that would eliminate two of them. His right hand shot toward the sky and then dropped over the arm of the chair. He moved it again and it landed on the arm. His fingers brushed the plastic buttons that controlled the genera-tors.

"Ssss . . . tttt . . . oppp. . . ."

The sec stopped. The cops got out of the car and stepped in front of the wheelchair. One of them held the dog on a u-shaped leash. The other one held out his hand.

"May I see your identification, please?"

"You making an arrest?" the sec said.

"We're just making a routine check."

"We don't have to."

"Don't have to what?" the cop with the dog said.

"You have to arrest us for something. No arrest, no ID."

The cop's face hardened. The grinning dog bobbed across Nicholson's vision. The thick muscle in his mouth quivered.

8

"Aaaaaag . . . verrr . . . gggggg. . . ."

"What are you doing here?" the cop with the dog said. "Who sent you here?"

The sec kept his mouth shut. A bony hand jerked the dog's leash. The dog growled.

"You want us to run you and your friend in for disturbing the peace, little boy?"

"We aren't making noise. You have to make a noise."

"You're a real lawyer, aren't you?"

His fingers were still resting on the buttons that controlled the generators. He could surprise them with a blast of almost anything, from the rear of a rocket to the smell of horse manure, and then hit them with the scrambler and run. The sec would know what he wanted as soon as he started waving the scrambler. Nobody would ever know he had run out right at the start of the project. If they ever got him in the station house and worked on him with a hypno. . . .

"Get them out of here," a man yelled. "Don't take any back talk."

All over the block people started yelling at them.

"Send them back where they came from."

"Sic the dog on 'em!"

The cop gestured at the excited people. "You aren't disturbing the peace?"

A little girl ran toward them across the nearest lawn. "Go away, bad man! Go away! Bad man! Bad man! Bad man!" Her mother yelled at her but she kept on coming. She stumbled over a drainage ditch at the end of the lawn and fell on the sidewalk.

Her mother screamed. The girl lifted her face off the sidewalk and screamed at him through her tears. Her mother ran across the lawn, yelling as if her child had been run over by a truck, and bent over her.

His hand dropped toward his lap and came up again. The mother glared at him and she picked up the girl. "There, there. Come in the house now. I'll give you some candy. We'll go in the house and we'll eat some of the candy Granddaddy sent us. It's all right. The man'll go away very soon."

The dog growled again. "Who are you working for?"

9

the cop said. "Who sent you here? Can't you see what these people think about spies?"

The sec drew himself up. The cops glanced at each other. The cop holding the dog grinned. "Let him do what he wants," the cop said. "It's a free country."

They trudged back to their car. Nicholson watched them climb into the front seat and waited for them to move. They smiled back at him and he realized they were going to stay right where they were. The people standing on the lawns looked like they were setting up a gauntlet.

"Ggggg . . . goooo . . . aaaaaa . . . aaaaaannnn. . . ."

The sec pushed him forward. Grown men and women screamed at him like angry children.

"Snooper!"

"Spy!"

"Go back to your garbage pit!"

The cops followed him down the block. His eyes took in everything but his brain refused to produce any insights. He took it all in: the people, the elaborate toys, the houses, the food and amusements scattered on blankets and lawn tables; and even as it flowed through his nervous system his brain planned escape routes and what he would do if they attacked. The Lone Knight was too scared to function. The kids back at the Saturday matinee were going to start booing any minute.

"Stop him! Don't let him go any farther!"

A girl jumped in front of the wheelchair. *"Don't let him poison our brains!* He's spying on our brains so they can sell us more garbage! Don't let him do it! Stop him! Stop him!"

The sec tried to push the chair around her. She threw out her arms and stepped back. She danced down the street in front of the chair.

"It's just like that milk company in Chicago. I saw it on television. They had a lot of bad milk and they worked on people's minds and made them buy it. Don't let them do it here! Don't let them stuff their junk down our throats!"

A black dress swirled around her body. Flickering lights from two computer-controlled jewels in her collar—a popular type of cosmetic—played on her face and bathed her features in swiftly changing patterns of light and shadow. Her breasts seemed oddly large on her thin body.

"He'll fix us so we have to buy his junk! He'll work on our minds! He'll stuff it down our throats! Don't you care what they do to you? Don't you want to be free?"

People moved toward him across the lawns. A small crowd gathered around the chair. The sec tried to push through and then stopped.

Faces swung past Nicholson's eyes. His tongue quivered. His hands appeared in front of his eyes and he pulled them down. Somewhere in the crowd he could hear music with a strong rhythm and a loud, thumping bass beat. A young rock was holding a plastic case that looked like an oversize portable radio. The rhythm was exactly the same as the rhythm of the lights moving over the girl's face.

A woman screamed at him from the back of the crowd. A man swore. Fists clenched. The fat man sucked on his cigar at the edge of his lawn.

"Kill him!" a woman yelled. "Kill him! Tear him to pieces! Show him what we do to snoops!"

Boom. Boom. Boom, boom, boom.

A blond young rock smiled and edged forward through the crowd. The girl danced in front of him like a hysterical child. His right hand slid toward the chair and the buttons that controlled the generators. He could almost control his muscles if he made small movements. The cops would haul him in for assault with a deadly weapon if he used the scrambler or the psycho-active gas bombs before they attacked him, and he would be lucky if half of them moved away if he generated a bad odor or a painful noise. Sound and scent had to be used with precision. If he tried to use them in a situation in which he didn't know his target, he might generate a stimulus that would reinforce the girl's rabble rousing. Even if he managed to break them up temporarily, how could he keep them from chasing him?

The girl drew herself up and pointed her finger at

11

him. She towered over him with her back arched and her swollen breasts standing up.

"Forget about the cops! The cops won't stop you. They don't want him to poison our minds either. Teach him a lesson! Don't let him stuff his junk down our throats! Do you want him coming back again?"

Men glanced at each other. They were still hesitating. They were making a lot of noise, but they weren't used to violence.

A boy slithered between two sets of legs. He stopped in front of the wheelchair and looked at Nicholson with the cruel face of a child mocking the village idiot. He was carrying a huge ice cream cone, three red-streaked scoops of vanilla piled in a high, dripping tower.

"How do you eat, mister? Show me how you eat."

Nicholson opened his mouth. His tongue quivered. The boy shoved the ice cream cone across his lap and he started and moved his left hand. The ice cream shot out of the boy's fingers and splattered on the sidewalk. The boy stepped back and brought up his hands as if he was warding off a blow.

A woman yelled. The boy wailed. The girl's voice rose above the crowd.

"Show him!" *Boom.* "Teach him!" *Boom.* "He's poisoning our brains! He's poisoning our brains!" *Boom. Boom. Boom, boom, boom.*

A hand grabbed his shirt collar. Faces moved toward him. Eyes stared at him over cigarettes and slowly chewing jaws. More than half the people here were smoking. Most of the rest were chewing gum.

A hard, masculine hand slapped his face hard enough to make his eyes water. He moaned and instantly felt ashamed. The hand drew back and balled into a fist and his right hand tightened its grip on the chair arm. Less than fifteen percent of the people in the crowd should have been smokers. Most of them were young enough to have reached their teens after the big anti-smoking campaigns of the seventies. Why would there be more smokers in Greenplace than in the almost identical development he had surveyed last week?

The fist dropped. The blows snapped his head back

and then forward, past the blue sky, the working jaws, the lips sucking on cigarettes, the surgically enlarged breasts of the girl, the people edging toward the chair, the fat bodies—the boy had deliberately moved his hand so he would knock the ice cream out of it!—the lawns, the houses like big, soft, edible. . . .

Orals!

They were all orals. Everyone in Greenplace was an oral.

"Teach him! Teach him! Kill him! Tear him apart!"

Questions and insights flashed through his brain. How could every person in a development this big belong to one psychological type? Could even Boyd's organization be that powerful? No wonder they had jumped him when he was only a block in. This must be one of the best kept secrets they had. Send in your psych technicians knowing everybody could be manipulated with one kind of appeal and. . . .

Ads and appeals raced past his eyes as if they were being projected on a screen. Pain and noise reached him through a torrent of thoughts. No cautious modern psychologist would have explained personality types with Freud's theories of infant development, but it was still true there were patterns of behavior that fitted Freud's terminology. Millions of Americans were dominated by the emotions associated with sucking and eating and the full, distended belly; drinkers, smokers, big consumers, people who ate when they were tense and anxious, lovers who tended to stimulate their sex partners with their mouths instead of their hands, compulsive talkers, running words through their mouths like streams of milk, adults who let off their anger and aggression screaming like children, hungry introverts devouring books and entertainment. Study a human being with any two or three traits and you would find a dozen of the hundred other traits that could make up the pattern. *See Boyd laugh. Watch Boyd eat. Boyd is warm and good-humored. Fill your house with good things. Live a full life. Vote for Martin Boyd.*

They were pulling him out of the chair. He could feel blood running down the side of his face. The hysterical beat of the music was reaching his consciousness through a ringing ear.

He pointed the finger with the scrambler at the man who was pulling him out of the chair. Confusion and disorientation distorted the man's face. He screamed and stumbled backward into the people pressing behind him.

The sec made a strange sound behind him. His drugged mind raced ahead at full speed. The second blow had hit his face only a few seconds ago.

His fingers wiggled on the buttons of the control panel. Formula eighty-two. Only two digits. Each button had a different texture, a scheme he had worked out to help him use the generator while he was drugged. Two tiny points pricked his finger and he pushed in the eight.

He waved the scrambler in wide, sweeping arcs. A rabbit punch sent pain shooting up his left arm. Hands grabbed his shoulders and shoved him forward and up. His forefinger slid across the smooth, hemispheric surface of the two button.

Twenty voices screamed with pleasure. A fist hit him in the stomach. A hand grabbed his arm and spun him around. Pain made him close his eyes. Somebody kicked him in the ankle. He opened his eyes and saw the sec fighting with a strange smile on his face.

The smell of human vomit filled the summer air.

A dozen voices gagged simultaneously. The hands gripping his body let him go. He fell back and hit the ground, waving his arms like a baby. All around him people pressed their hands against their faces and stumbled away from the chair with their backs bent double. A girl closed her eyes and fainted. A man old enough to be his father tripped over the edge of the sidewalk and lay on the grass gagging. Retching, swearing people stampeded across the lawns.

The sec's big body blocked out the sky. Strong arms pulled him up and shoved him into the wheelchair. Wheels rumbled on the sidewalk. The girl jumped in front of them waving her arms and jumped back when the sec nearly ran her down. Even she looked sick.

II

HE KNEW SUE had been worried as soon as he entered the apartment. She had taken off the slacks and blouse outfit she had been wearing when he had left and put on an outfit she usually only wore when she went out: a calf-length, orange version of an African toga, that set off her black hair and fair skin and made her look as dignified as a queen. She could endure almost anything, she claimed, if she could face it feeling dignified and well-dressed.

His four-year-old daughter, Nancy, ran across the living room yelling daddee. He squatted on the floor and pulled her into his arms. Clean female hair brushed against the side of his face. His two year old, Ellen, jumped up and down beside him and yelled.

He picked up Ellen and stood up. She watched him from the kitchen door. His six year old, Lorin, smiled at him from the painting she was working on, and he waved jauntily and smiled back. He couldn't look at Sue. He could feel every bruise and scratch on his face glowing like a neon sign under all the work the technicians in the cosmetic room at the hospital had done on him during the forty-five minutes they had worked on his face.

Nancy pulled on his leg. "You have to see the thing I made. Come on, daddy."

She ran across the room backward. He bounced Ellen in his arms and followed her. "How did it go?" Sue said.

"I'll tell you later."

He looked down at the thing Nancy had made with her latest construction set. It looked like a square tower with a dome on top and some kind of walled area around it.

"That looks very interesting, love. Is there any chance you can tell me what it is?"

Nancy squatted on the floor. She turned a gear and

15

the dome started turning. A plastic fish shape slid out of a door and circled the walled area and she looked up. She had her mother's glossy hair and her mother's bright, intelligent eyes, and he had a feeling she was going to be more like her mother than any of them. They were all slender, intelligent girls but Nancy already had that extra little liveliness that had made him fall in love with Sue and with half the other girls he had ever fallen in love with. She wasn't as pretty as Rachel or Lorin, and she wasn't as intelligent as Margaret, but he could see her striding through life with that extra intensity that made everything Sue did seem twice as exciting as it should have.

"It's an apartment house for some astronomer whales," Nancy said. "They're studying the stars so they can navigate better."

Ellen wiggled in his arms. "Ellen help. Ellen help."

He bent over and scrubbed Nancy's hair with his palm. He could feel the pressure he was under working on every organ in his body.

"That's exactly what I thought it was. Excuse me a minute while I make a phone call, love. I'll be right back."

Nancy jumped up and grabbed his arm. "You said you were going to play!"

He put Ellen on the floor and straightened up. "I'll be right back."

"You said you'd play as soon as you got home. You promised."

She threw her arms around his leg and pressed her face against his thigh. The beginning of a tantrum twisted her face.

Sue's hands cracked like a pistol shot. "Leave daddy alone! Let him make his phone call!"

He hurried down the hall to his bedroom with a four-year-old voice wailing behind his back. The bedroom door slid shut behind him and he turned toward the life-size phone screen mounted on the wall.

"Computer. Call Dr. Robert Dazella in Washington, D.C."

The screen blinked twice. Dazella's name and phone

number appeared in the lower right-hand corner and the phone started buzzing at the other end.

He waited with his hands clasped behind his back. He was a tall, thin man, and Sue claimed he oscillated between two postures; either he was sprawled all over a chair or he was standing up and pacing the floor like a sailing captain on the deck of a ship.

Dazella's ugly, big-browed face jumped onto the screen. His eyes scanned Nicholson's body as if he were reading a report from one of his subordinates.

"I see you survived anyway," Dazella said. "How did it go?"

"I ran into a little opposition. They set a mob on me and I had to break it up."

"The bastards don't waste any time, do they? Did they hurt anything important?"

"I got some minor bruises. I put in a couple of hours at the hospital so Sue wouldn't run away from me when I came home, but I think I came out ahead. I stumbled over a little secret of theirs while I was under the drug."

"You found something you can use already?"

"It could come in handy sooner or later. It's a little grisly, but it's the kind of thing we can turn around and use against them now that we know it's there."

"Is it so important to them they may try to have me assassinated if you break down and actually tell me some of the details?"

"I rechecked the phone for taps this morning. They already know I know about it anyway."

"You may as well let me know about it, too. The more people know about it, the less reason they'll have to shut you up."

It had been a long time since he had seen Dazella look shocked. Lincoln had once said any man over forty was responsible for his face, and he could have used Dazella as supporting evidence. Dazella was a successful businessman and political organizer partly because he was a tough-minded man who could accept most of the realities without flinching. They had been working together for five years now and they had used

17

psych techniques in both the campaigns that had put Dazella in the House of Representatives.

"It's a very economical gimmick," Nicholson said. "One area, one type, and they can hit everybody with the same kind of stimulus. They can work on the damned place every day if they want to and never have to worry about the stimulus that works on one voter and turns his next door neighbor against them. They can probably sample one percent of the people in the area and come up with the same results they'd get if they sampled everybody."

Dazella shook his head. "I knew the bastards had come a long way but I'll be Goddamned if I thought they'd gotten that far."

"It wouldn't even have occurred to me if I hadn't been drugged."

"How the hell could they set a thing like that up in five years? Some of those people must have lived in that damned place since the seventies. Boyd may have started playing around with psych techniques before John Hill started working for him but I'll be damned if I can believe he could have come up with something like that himself."

"I thought about that on the way home. They could have had a high proportion of this particular G-type living there to start with. The houses are built so they'd appeal to this type. Hill could have noticed it and started slanting the advertising for the place so it would up the percentage. He could have had fifty or sixty percent when he started. I'd say it's about ninety-five percent successful right now."

"And you're still willing to go back there?"

"After this? If this doesn't convince some of our friends these bastards have to be brought down, nothing will."

"This was only supposed to be a probe, remember? What the hell do you think they'll have waiting for you next time if they can set up a situation like the one they've got in that development? I know how these people think, Ralph. I'm not trying to talk you into backing out of this, but this is no time to get locked into it either. A little incident like this is all the evidence a guy like Boyd needs. He knows you're definitely a threat now. He'll hit you with everything he's got and try to crush you before you get bigger."

"He tried that today," Nicholson said. "This is no time to get overconfident, but they didn't exactly prove they can't be beaten either. This is the first time Hill's had to operate in a situation where somebody's trying to push people left while he's trying to push them right. If he'd ever thought he might have to face another political organization armed with psych techniques, he wouldn't have set a thing like Greenplace up. That's the kind of gimmick that only makes sense when you don't have to worry about somebody else finding out about it and using it against you. I turned it against them today and I can turn it against them when we start a campaign, too."

"That still doesn't mean you can come out of this thing in one piece if Boyd decides they should focus everything they've got on you personally. I'm afraid I've got some news for you, too, Ralph. It isn't quite as upsetting as yours, but don't convince yourself you have to keep this up before you've heard it."

Nicholson tensed. There was a bottle of twenty-minute tranquilizers on the shelf over the bed and it was beginning to look as attractive as his bottle had probably looked when he had been a baby.

"I may as well get it all in one day. What are they doing to the world now?"

"I had a long talk with one of my friends in the Philadelphia organization the other day and he told me something I'd never heard before. He called me up because a couple of Boyd's people had been asking questions about you, and I told him you were worried about the possibility they might psych you and asked him if he'd give them some false information for us. He told me he didn't think it would make a damn bit of difference. Boyd isn't limited to keeping tabs on people in his district. He can probably get his hands on anything the central computers in the census bureau can pull out of the federal files. He can't do it often, but he can do it now and then if he wants the information bad enough."

Nicholson's heart jumped. He straightened up before he could get his emotions under control and Dazella scanned him again. He could have typed himself with one glance at the personal biography the census bureau could put together from all the records stored in the federal computers. It would only have been a guess, but any competent psychologist could have verified it in two or three days without his subject even knowing he was being tested.

"I probably should have told you about it before I let you go back there," Dazella said. "I didn't corner the guy who could really verify it's true until this morning and I didn't want you to go back there with something like that in the back of your mind if it wasn't true. I can't prove it to you, but don't kid yourself into thinking it isn't true. Nobody came up to me and told me Boyd's people made him tell them how to get around the locks on the computers. But I talked to two people I trust beside the guy I talked to this morning and they all told me they're convinced it's true. I wouldn't make another move if I were you without assuming he's got you typed and taking it into consideration. You're the strategic point in the whole project, Ralph. Once he finds out you're the only psychologist on the other side he'll go after you with the biggest guns he's got."

The haze between Nicholson and the screen disappeared. The part of his personality that monitored his emotions smiled wryly. He wasn't reacting like this because he was afraid they would psych him. He had known they would probably type him when he had started this; the census records would make it easy for them, but there were a dozen other ways they could do it if they wanted to spend the money. He was cringing like a cornered animal because a few more people were going to learn Ralph Nicholson was a human being with human emotions and human drives. He had been typed ever since he had enrolled in graduate school in 1980—dozens of people knew the basic structure of his personality—but the old reflexes still leaped into action every time he learned somebody new might be added to the mob.

20

He shook his head. "I should have known the bastards could do something like that. Give them another twenty years and they'll be running the country like it's a damned push-button toy."

"Forget the damned country. Give them another month and they may be running you."

"It doesn't make that much difference. I knew they could type me when they started this. They could probably put a round the clock crew on me and keep me under surveillance for six months if they had to, with the kind of organization they've got. I've only got two defenses against psych attacks that really count. I know what kind of techniques they'll probably use and I've got Ed Saboletsky backing me up. I talked to Ed on Thursday and he finally gave in. I'm supposed to call him once a week and get an hour long psych check. He'll call you right away if he thinks they've been working on me and he's supposed to call me any time he hears something unusual has happened to me."

"What if they do something to you he can't detect?"

"I picked Ed Saboletsky because he's the best therapist I know and because he thinks any successful psychologist who gets involved in politics should have his own psychology examined by a select committee of the American Psychological Association. He's so worried about me he'll probably think I've been psyched if I call one of my daughters by the wrong name."

"What if they do something to you that can't be repaired?"

"What are you trying to do, Robert, scare me? We talked about that the first time I told you I wanted to do this, damnit. I can sit down right now and work out four different ways they could condition me so I'd become a nervous wreck every time I went near Windham County. I got a first hand look at the risks I'm running three hours ago, remember?"

Dazella scowled. A child screeched in one of the other rooms and Nicholson's muscles tensed as if somebody had sounded the buzzer that was supposed to precede the electric shock. He was supposed to take Sue to a big party tonight and Nancy was probably going to pounce on him as soon as he left the bedroom. A twenty-minute chemical vacation would make a big difference.

"Do me two favors, Ralph," Dazella said. "I can't talk you out of going ahead with this if you really want to. And I'm not sure I really want you to stop anyway. But use a car next time, Goddamnit. And for God's sake, quit making excuses about taking self-defense instruction. I've been talking to the head man at the dojo Peggy studies karate at and and I think we've come up with something you can use. Have you ever heard of the little stick, the six-inch stick?"

Nicholson shook his head. He was a rare creature in this day and age; he had never studied karate, aikido, or jujitsu. He had wanted to learn a practical self-defense system ever since he had been a kid but he had been too busy when he had been a student and he had never gotten around to it since then.

Dazella reached inside his jacket and pulled out a white plastic stick. "It's just a little stick like this. You use it just like you use the fist or the open hand in karate. You strike at the nerve centers and the pain centers with the ends of the stick. The big difference is that you can learn to use it in a lot less time than it takes you to learn karate. You can practice in between patients in your office if you want to. You'll need an hour of general instruction—they can give you that over the phone—and you can buy a practice dummy and work out by yourself after that. They've got a dummy that sells for five hundred dollars. It comes with a complete programmed course and they claim they can modify the course to suit your schedule. You can put the program in your office computer and plug the dummy into the computer with a single plug."

Dazella's right hand rose above his shoulders. He stabbed at an invisible target in front of him as if he were holding a knife. "Chin . . . solar plexus . . . side of the neck . . . eyes. . . . You can kill somebody with this thing if you know what to do with it. Half the people in the country would be using them if everybody hadn't gotten hooked on the other unarmed arts first."

22

"What happens if I don't happen to have a little white stick with me?"

"They cost about five dollars a dozen. You can carry one stuck in your belt under your jacket anywhere you go and nobody'll ever notice it."

"Just like a well-trained agent for the Japanese Board of Trade."

"It's one of the handiest defense systems the Japanese ever came up with. I made Peggy take it up when she started studying karate and I've never regretted the extra money it cost me."

"Can they give me the one-hour lesson tomorrow morning at ten?"

"The head man at the dojo will call you himself. I'll call him right away. I had him put the whole order on standby."

"I always did want to feel like a well-dressed hoodlum."

"Thank God for something. If I had any sense I'd probably have you kidnapped and condition you into staying away from that damned place myself."

"I wouldn't put it past you, Robert. Do you have any more little tidbits?"

"*Don't be afraid to quit, damnit.* Don't get irrational about this. Nobody will ever hold it against you if you quit."

"I'll consider the idea seriously every time it occurs to me."

"If we had any sense, we'd both probably be considering a few good old-fashioned assassinations."

"Or a one-way trip to the moon."

"The bastards will probably be pushing buttons up there in a few years, too. I'll see you later, Ralph. Call me right away if you need any help."

"I'll let you know as soon as anything significant happens. Let me know if you get any good bribes."

"I'll send you your usual commission."

He stepped across the room and reached for the tranquilizers as soon as the screen blanked. Somebody knocked on the door and he turned around with one of the pills in his palm.

"Who is it?"

"Your wife."

He hesitated with the pill in his hand. He had called Dazella first partly because he had wanted to put off talking to Sue.

He forced the pill down his throat and put the jar back on the shelf.

"Come in, love. Come in."

The door slid open as he turned around. She slipped inside and they eyed each other across the room.

"I thought I'd better talk to you alone," Sue said. "Do you still feel like taking Nancy to the fun house?"

"Sure. I've been assuming she'll be ready to go as soon as I get my clothes changed."

"I told her you might not. She was very brave about it."

The tranquilizer flowed through Nicholson's consciousness. Muscles relaxed all over his body. A thick, mushy wall rose between him and his emotions.

"I just wanted to talk to Bob Dazella first. I knew he'd want to hear how it went right away."

"You looked like you had an interesting day when you came in."

A numb guilt about the tranquilizer penetrated the mushy wall. She would have taken a tranquilizer herself if she had been in his position but that didn't change things. He was hiding inside a shelter and she was out in the open.

"I ran into a little trouble. It didn't do me any great harm personally, but I stumbled on something that really caught me off guard."

"They tried to stop you already?"

"That's only part of it. You may want to change your mind about helping me when you hear the rest of it."

"The first time anything happens?"

"They're doing something that took me completely by surprise. It isn't quite as bad as it looks at first sight, but it isn't the kind of thing I like to think about late at night either. It even shocked Bob."

"It must be pretty awful if it even shocked him. What are they doing—organizing a campaign to make people hate Italian politicians?"

"They tried to set a mob on me. They stirred up

24

the mob with a gimmick they've got and I managed to figure out the gimmick while I was under the drug and turn it against them. I had to stop at the hospital on the way back and get a few bruises wiped off but I managed to figure out the gimmick and stop the show before they did anything serious. The main thing is the damned gimmick. They've set up a surburban development in which every damned personality in the area is the same Gruber type—every man, woman, and child in a place that must have two thousand people in it."

Her eyes widened. Her hand moved toward her mouth as if she were a twenty-year-old ingenue.

"There's no doubt about it," Nicholson said. "I had the sec push me all over the Goddamned area after we got away from them, and you can look at the stuff scattered on the lawn and see it, once you know what to look for. I used a noise and odor stimulus that's guaranteed to work on this particular G-type and every personality in the mob responded like I was putting on a demonstration in the classroom."

"They've gotten that far? They're pushing people around like that?"

"It looks like an organization with that much money and power can do almost anything it Goddamn wants to nowadays. I'm not trying to talk you out of helping me, love, but it looks like you're going to be in a lot more danger than we thought you'd be. We can't assume you'll be safe just because you're supposed to stay on this side of the Delaware River most of the time."

He settled his shoulder against the wall and watched her adjust to it as if he were dealing with a patient. He would be very surprised if she backed out of this now that she had agreed to do it. She had argued with him for two months when he had told her he wanted her to help him with this project, but now that she was committed to it, he was certain she would fight for her personal freedom with the same hunger with which she had fought for everything else she had ever wanted. She had hated the advertising work she had been doing when he had first met her, but she

25

had gone on doing it because it had been the only trade in which she could pull down an upper middle class salary and enjoy the life style that went with it. She had been a hungry young woman who had wanted everything the world had to offer, and her appetite had been so strong she had been willing to satisfy it with weapons that revolted her. And now that she knew people like Boyd were threatening her freedom, he was certain she would go after Boyd's throat with the same intensity with which she had gone after all the baubles on the Christmas tree.

"Every single person in that place is the same type, every member of every family?"

"It looked to me like they managed to attract mono-type couples most of the time. They can't control the kids that closely, but people with this type of personality tend to establish a family pattern that molds their kids into the same type."

"And they can hire some clever little ad maker and have her zero in right on that one spot, knowing she can ignore the side effects and come up with something that's exactly right for every damned person there."

"Right."

"And you think I'd quit on you now that we know we're dealing with people who can do something like that?"

"You decided you'd help me when we thought they were a lot less powerful than it looks like they really are. I'd be pretty damned surprised if you quit anything you started. But this isn't the project you volunteered for."

"I'm not going to drop out on you right at the start. I may not have whatever it takes to last the whole distance, but I'm not going to drop out now."

The numb guilt about the tranquilizer penetrated the chemical wall again. She would have looked like she was chatting with a guest at a party if anybody had taken a picture of her, but he knew he would have picked up the odors of fear if he had been spying on her with an odor detector.

He moved toward her mechanically. The tranquilizer was still numbing his emotions, but he had been living with himself for forty-four years now and he could usually play the part from memory.

"It's up to you, love. It's a filthy thing to ask your own wife to help you with, but I'd rather have you working with me than anybody else that's ever been in the business."

III

ALBERT MEAD LIVED in one of the richest developments in the Fifth Congressional District—a sprawling complex in which all the houses were built on small islands and electric boats hummed along a complicated network of canals and lakes. The houses looked like they probably cost a million to buy and fifty a year to maintain and the land around them was crowded with proof that the developer had used every modern technique that would add to their value. Birds squawked above the water with voices that had been selected by behavioral psychologists and built into their physiology by genetic engineers. Specially designed fish and water animals splashed in the canals. Plants bloomed and faded in a constantly changing, custom-made pattern that had been programmed by the best ecologists and genetic engineers in the northeast. Air purifiers and specially designed plants kept the air fresh and clean in spite of the presence of enormous sources of pollution only a few miles away.

The developer's commercials claimed the development was a "pure, controlled landscape only a few miles from a major modern city. A home in Country Islands is like a time machine that takes you back to the unspoiled countryside of the eighteenth century." And Nicholson had to admit the commercials were almost right. Only the sky reminded him he was still in Windham County, New Jersey, at the beginning of the twenty-first century. The human eye could see stars of the sixth magnitude when the air was truly clean, but the dimmest stars above his head were stars of the third

27

magnitude. The developer could clean the air seventy feet above a limited area, but the air above that was just as dirty as it had been when he had been a young dandy in the eighties.

He hummed along the canals with the top down and sucked in the chilly autumn air that always reminded him of the first semester of school and all the Octobers and Novembers in which he had worked in political campaigns. Music reached him from half the islands he passed. Winged, propeller-driven "fireworks" soared above the development, with their lights weaving patterns in the sky. A pleasure boat loaded with singing men and women pulled up beside him and a woman threw a cornstalk at him and curtsied in her seat when he automatically raised the stalk to his lips and blew a kiss at her. For fifteen years now the people who sold party gadgets and fancy clothes had been gradually turning the autumn into a festival that stretched from early October to the beginning of the Christmas season on Thanksgiving Day. People danced and sang and gorged themselves on big meals, as if the harvest really was a brief interlude of plenty, and the winter was really going to bring cold and hunger instead of a festival that was even bigger. He would have been singing himself if Sue had been with him and he had been paying a social call.

The automatic guidance system picked up Albert Mead's landing code. The taxi boat slipped through the traffic and turned toward a medium-sized island and a simple, two-story house that had been sculptured out of glass and shiny white plastic. A white plastic wall surrounded most of the island and a rocky path connected the front gate with the house.

The boat eased up to the landing. The bow swung back and forth as the guidance system positioned the hull beside the steps. The boat stopped two inches from the landing and Nicholson stood up.

A loudspeaker murmured beside his chair. "We have arrived at the home of Dr. Albert Mead. Please be careful when you disembark. Please call for a taxi ten minutes before you are ready to leave."

Nicholson stepped onto the landing. A light blinked

beside a television camera above the gate and he turned toward it and let the people inside the house see his face.

A motorboat swerved toward him out of the darkness. Three young rocks piled out of it while it was still moving and jumped onto the landing. His taxi turned around ten feet from the landing and hummed down the river toward its next call.

Two rocks jumped between Nicholson and the gate before he could move. Two arrogant young faces smiled at him. The delicate odor of violet perfume spread across the dock.

His hands rose toward his belt. The rocks were all shorter than he was but their hands looked big and hard.

The third rock posed on the edge of the dock with his hands on his hips. He was a little older than the other two and his balanced, stocky body looked like it had been shaped by years of judo and karate.

"Happy Halloween, psychman. Meet your new teachers. We're going to give you a little lesson in staying away from the Fifth Congressional District of the state of New Jersey, and we're going to use the best principles of psychology to do it. First we tell you what you're supposed to learn. Then we give you a little reinforcement to help you remember it."

The two rocks in front of the gate stepped forward. He turned his head and the other rock skipped toward him.

A punch jarred his side. He pulled his scrambler out of his belt with his left hand and jerked the stick out of its holster with his right. The older rock started to hit him again and he swung at the incoming arm with his stick and waved his scrambler at the other two.

The stick stabbed into a forearm. The two rocks he had swept with the scrambler gasped and fell back with their hands over their faces. His reflexes swung the scrambler toward the third rock.

Somebody splashed into the water. The older rock swung as he brought the scrambler around and a fist slammed into his heart. An edge of the hand blow

29

jarred his left arm. The scrambler flew out of his fingers.

His right hand snapped back to his waist and shot out. The stick rammed into stomach muscle. The rock doubled over and he pulled his hand back and struck him in the side of the head.

The rock sank to one knee. He clutched his head with his hands and Nicholson stepped back and looked down at him with his guard wide open. He had never knocked a man down before.

The gate opened half a foot. A voice boomed out of a loudspeaker. "Get inside! Hurry!"

The rock who had stumbled into the water was clutching the landing and staring up at him defiantly. The rock he had hit with the stick had slipped to both knees and looked like he might be getting ready to keel over. The third rock was leaning against the wall with his hands on his face.

The gate swung open another foot as he stepped toward it. It slammed home as soon as he squeezed through it and the older rock raised his head and stared at him through the iron bars.

The rock who had stumbled into the water crawled onto the landing. The other two rocks stood up and eyed Nicholson through the gate.

The rock who had stumbled into the water stood up and pushed back his hair. Water ran down his waterproof clothes as if they had been made out of Sheetrock.

"I should have known a cancer like you would use a Goddamned scrambler. Don't push your luck, psychman. Next time we'll know what to watch for."

"This is a bad place to come, psychman. You're heading straight for a nice bed in the hospital."

Nicholson's hand gripped the gate. He stared back at them with the stick poised near his waist and the leader jerked around and stepped into the boat. The other two rocks climbed in after him and they skidded away from the landing and hummed down the canal with their fists raised.

Nicholson sagged against the gate. He had been waiting for something like this for three months, but they had still caught him by surprise.

He stuck the stick in its holster and straightened up. The clean air in his lungs felt as exhilarating as a drug. He had knocked a man down in a fair fight! They had attacked him by surprise and he had still managed to swing the stick like a veteran. The rock he had knocked down had looked like he was a trained fighter. And he had been twenty years younger, too.

His built-in monitor smiled wryly. He shook his head and pushed himself away from the gate.

A bald, heavy man hurried down the path with his hand out. "Are you all right, Dr. Nicholson? What's going on?"

Nicholson wiped the sweat off his forehead. He had talked to Albert Mead on the phone but this was the first time they had met in person."

"I'm fine. I was just stopping to get my nerve back."

"It looks like you really gave the little cancers a rough time."

"I had a scrambler with me."

"It looked like you clobbered one of them with your bare hands, too."

"I gave him a couple of taps with the little stick—the little six-inch stick the Japanese have a system for. Are you familiar with that?"

"That's what it was. It looked like you knew how to handle it."

"I put some money into a practice dummy a couple of months ago and got my reflexes programmed. The guy that sold me on it told me it's the easiest self-defense system you can learn and it looks like he was right."

"It's getting so you practically have to carry a damn gun around here. You didn't manage to get the license number of the little cancers' boat, did you?"

"I didn't even think about it."

"That's too bad. The cops may be able to track them down anyway, but it would be a hell of a lot easier if we had the license number."

Nicholson hesitated. The TV camera had probably been turned on when the rocks had jumped onto the

31

landing, but Mead could have missed the rock's first words. And Mead could have been heading for the door when the rocks had been shouting at him through the gate.

"I'd just as soon leave the cops out of it if we can do it. I'd rather not get involved in a lot of red tape."

"They won't keep you on the phone more than ten minutes. They aren't the most efficient cops in the United States but it's probably worth a try."

"I'd rather let it ride. I can't explain it right now without going into a lot of detail, but it has something to do with the reason I'm here."

Mead frowned. His eyes studied Nicholson's face. "You're sure? They jumped you because of that?"

"They made it pretty clear."

"Let's go inside."

A flute solo was rising toward a peak as they entered the house. A woman was leaning against a chair in the center of the living room and the wall behind her was filled with a life-size, three-dimensional broadcast of a ballet that was obviously being performed on the moon. Six dancers had just jumped twenty feet off the floor and a camera was tracking them from above as they glided down.

Mead gestured at the woman. "This is a friend of mine, Dr. Elaine Bruckner. This is Dr. Ralph Nicholson, Elaine. He got a little shook up out there but he claims he's still in one piece."

The woman slipped off the chair and came toward them with her hand out. She was a tall, bony blonde who looked like she might be in her middle thirties, and her lounging clothes and her general manner indicated she either lived in the house or spent most of her evenings there. Mead had been divorced twice, according to the records Nicholson had checked, and he had apparently slipped into the sexual pattern a lot of divorced men slipped into sooner or later.

"Thank God you're all right! I nearly died when I saw those little cancers jump out of that boat."

"It caught me off guard, too, I'm afraid. I hope it looked reasonably entertaining on the TV monitor."

"Thank Heaven you know how to protect yourself.

32

That's the second time I've seen something like that in two years."

"I thought my generation were terrors," Mead said. "Some of these kids nowadays don't care what they do."

"I'm just glad they weren't very competent," Nicholson said. "They stopped to say a few choice words and then they seemed surprised when I managed to get my scrambler out before they closed in."

"They probably thought you'd hesitate," Elaine Bruckner said. "I would have been so scared I probably wouldn't have moved."

Mead gestured at the bar on the side of the room. "How about picking up some medicine for your nerves before we go upstairs? I've got a good office on the second floor but I'm afraid I didn't have room for a bar after I got all the junk I need set up."

"That sounds like the best thing I've heard since I arrived in New Jersey. You wouldn't happen to have something pretty mild, would you? I usually stick to things like Schneider's Weingarden Number One these days."

"Is that one of the ones that tastes like a Moselle wine?"

"Right. The active ingredient is TP3L in one part in a hundred."

"How about Gallio's Mild Joy? It tastes a little more acid than a wine does but I think it's got the same stuff in the same concentration. I can give it to you mulled or on ice."

"That sounds fine. Ice'll be fine."

"I'll probably have the same thing myself. I usually like something stronger but if we're going to talk business . . ."

Elaine Bruckner stepped up to the bar and punched a couple of buttons on the control panel. Two glasses slid out of the chute and paused under a spout that loaded them with ice cubes and an amber liquid. She handed out the drinks with a little curtsy and Nicholson bowed back.

"We may as well go upstairs," Mead said. "I've been turning into a real ballet nut but we're taping that so I can look at it tomorrow."

Elaine picked up a drink and settled down in front of the screen. She tipped her drink at them as they started up the stairs and Nicholson tipped his drink back and followed Mead's big shoulders up an open staircase that looked like it belonged on a ship.

The office at the top of the stairs was equipped with a six screen computer console and a good selection of the other electronic equipment people like Mead used to run multimillion dollar businesses out of their homes. The black and orange armchairs were about fifteen years out of style but the rest of the equipment looked like it belonged to a man who traded in his old stuff as soon as something better came on the market.

Mead gestured at the chairs and turned on a switch near the door. Ballet music floated out of a pair of loudspeakers and he dropped into the swivel chair by the console.

"You can say anything you want in here," Mead said. "I've got some of the best antisnooping equipment you can buy in here. It came on automatically as soon as I entered the room and you'll see lights flashing all over the place if something in the system fails. The government won't let me do classified work here, but I've worked on some of the biggest accounts you can handle in my line of work and I haven't had a leak yet."

"This may be a good night to have something like that on your side," Nicholson said. "I don't know what kind of protection you've got in the rest of the house, but we'd probably better assume somebody's listening in on anything we say outside this room."

"You think the people who sent those rocks after you may be spying on you, too?"

"The rocks made it pretty clear who sent them. You probably didn't pick it up on your TV monitor, but they claimed they wanted to make sure I knew why they were beating me up."

"And they still didn't have the sense to know you probably had a scrambler in your belt? The guy that paid for that operation better get himself a new talent scout."

Nicholson hesitated. He'd been thinking about this meeting for the last three days but he still had to think before he talked. Every sentence in this conversation was like a move in a board game.

"It could have been a probe. I've been working on this project for three months now but they could still be feeling me out."

"A probe?"

"To find out how I react. I'm working on a project in which I may create some serious problem for people who use psych techniques every day. They wouldn't be running true to form if they didn't try to get my personality typed."

Mead shook his head. He tipped his glass at Nicholson and they raised their drinks and let the first drops of the tart amber liquid slide down their tongues.

"You sound a lot more nonchalant about the possibility you may be typed than I ever could," Mead said. "I don't want to insult your profession, Dr. Nicholson, but I feel like picking up a club and going berserk every time somebody reminds me I live in a world where people can fit me into a psychological pigeonhole and tell me what I'll be having for breakfast tomorrow."

Warm, pleasant sensations spread across Nicholson's skin. His muscles started relaxing and he settled back in his chair. The active ingredient in the happy drink had become his favorite relaxer during the last couple of years and it got better every time he used it. It calmed him down as well as most tranquilizers, and it did it without affecting his ability to think. It soothed his nerves by relaxing his muscles and stimulating tactile sensations that were normally associated with pleasure and calm.

"I don't like psychological manipulation any more than you do," Nicholson said. "Did you read the article I had in the *New York Times* magazine a couple of years ago?"

"I just read it two days ago. I looked it up after you called me up."

"Then you know exactly how I feel about psychological manipulation. I'm a therapist and I've been a therapist all my life. The political and commercial manipulation that's going on nowadays revolts me as much

35

as biological warfare revolts people who work in physical medicine. The ultimate goal of the project I'm working on is the destruction of one of the worst examples of psychological manipulation in the world today."

"You're actually trying to do something about the problem?"

"I'm trying to make a major attack on it—and I came here to ask you to give me some major help."

"And risk getting psyched myself?"

Nicholson smiled. "Right."

Mead shook his head again. The effects of the drug began to wear off and Nicholson automatically raised his drink and let a few drops slide down his tongue.

"I'm not trying to shock you," Nicholson said. "I came here to ask you to help me with a dangerous project. I wouldn't be doing either of us any good if I didn't tell you what the risks are right at the start. It isn't a suicide mission—I wouldn't do it if I didn't think there's a good chance it can succeed and we can all come out of it in one piece—but I wouldn't be honest if I didn't tell you there's a possibility somebody may try to foul you up psychologically."

"And I shouldn't let you go on unless I'm willing to take that kind of risk for the cause?"

"Right."

"How much of an effect do you really think you'll have on the problem?"

"There's a good chance we can completely eliminate political manipulation in some of the areas in which it's really gotten out of hand. There's a reasonable chance we can put a stop to it nationwide."

Mead's eyebrows rose. "You honestly think you can make people like Martin Boyd stop fooling around with our psyches?"

"There's a reasonable chance a lot of people like Boyd won't be in business when we get finished. I can't guarantee it, but the odds are good enough so I think it's worth trying."

"That sounds like a pretty ambitious undertaking."

"I'm working on a campaign to get Martin Boyd out of Congress and break up his organization. It's a very limited goal and it's going to take more guts than it looks like it's worth but it could have pretty important long-range results if we manage to pull it off. I've got some people backing me up financially who hate political manipulation as much as I do. If we manage to bring Boyd down, people will be launching attacks against other organizations like his."

"You think you can unseat the congressman who controls one of the strongest political organizations in the United States?"

"I've spent three months studying the problem. The evidence indicates Boyd can be defeated in the 2002 election if somebody makes the right moves."

"By a Republican? In Windham County?"

"Right."

"In thirteen months?"

"The Republican candidate can beat him if the Republicans put up the right kind of candidate and the candidate makes the right moves during the campaign. It isn't a sure thing, but we've got a reasonable chance."

"And you want me to help you?"

"I've got all the financial support the project needs. I can't go into any details but I've got enough money to pull it off if I get a normal amount of support from people inside the district. Boyd's a powerful man nationally, but a lot of people would like to get him out of Congress, and some of them are willing to slip the right people some cash if they can do it without Boyd knowing it. And I've also got some support from people who want to do something about psych manipulation and who feel this is a good place to start. If a rich, powerful organization like Boyd's can be broken up, then the other organizations that are starting to use psych techniques can be broken up, too—and we'll be getting rid of a committee chairman who's one of the biggest obstacles to laws that would bring psych manipulation under control."

Mead slumped back in his chair and shook his head. The music on the loudspeakers stopped for a moment and then a flute and a harp started playing something evocative and otherworldly.

"I've been living in this damned county for fifteen years," Mead said. "And this is the first time anybody who claims he knows anything about politics has ever tried to tell me Martin Boyd could be defeated in a congressional election. I'm certain you know what you're talking about, Dr. Nicholson. But I got involved in an attempt to unseat Boyd five years ago. You're going to have a lot of trouble convincing people who've seen that organization in operation."

"Every political expert in the United States agrees Boyd is unbeatable. And he would be, under normal circumstances. Nobody with real money or real political appeal is going to waste his time fighting an organization like Boyd's. If anybody in this area happens to be politically ambitious, he's either going to leave the area or he's going to join Boyd's organization and climb up inside it. I've spent three months building up a model of the country, however. And the results prove Boyd can be defeated by the right candidate. My model isn't as good as the model Boyd's psych experts use but it's good enough for me to say that. He probably would have been defeated five years ago if he hadn't started using psych techniques. He's got all the money and power you can accumulate when you've been a national political figure for forty-eight years, but he's got his share of weaknesses, too. He's operating in an area that has a very mobile, very middle class population, and you can't stay in office in that kind of area just by getting a lot of support from the local political crowd. You have to really win the voters over, too. The money and the support are only useful if you can use them to mount a campaign that will really make the voters buy you. Boyd is working under a big handicap every time he runs. He's not the kind of man most of the voters around here really want. He's at least twenty years too old, for one thing. And his record on a lot of issues is all wrong, too. His psych people have to work like galley slaves every time he runs. Put him up against a candidate who's been chosen because he has maximum appeal, and there's a real chance a well-run campaign can knock him right out of office. And once he's lost his seat in Congress, there's a good chance his organization may start to fall apart, too."

Mead's eyes narrowed. He pulled in a few drops of his happy drink and Nicholson waited while he rolled them around on his tongue.

"This is pretty good stuff," Mead said. "I'll have to start drinking it more often."

"I think it's the perfect drink for this kind of situation," Nicholson said. "It doesn't interfere with your brain and it relaxes you so much you probably actually think better."

"You're building up a psych model? You're basing all these predictions you're making on a psych model?"

"I made some shoestring surveys of the district and I filled in the rest of the details with general sociological data. I can't build up a model that's as detailed as Boyd's model, but I know my predictions of the potential vote are already correct within ten percent— and that means the right candidate can win by at least a three percent margin if he makes the right moves."

"And your model of the county will tell him the right moves? You'll pit your model against his model and the man you pick for a candidate will twist himself into whatever kind of shape the computer picks for him?"

"It's the only way it can be done," Nicholson said. "It took me half a year to make up my mind and I spent another couple of months arguing about it with some of the other people I've been working with. And we all came to the same conclusion. It's the only way anybody can break these organizations up. Nothing else will do it, and we may not have another chance if we don't start working on it now."

"You've given the problem all that thought and you can't come up with a way to attack them without using the same kind of poison they use?"

"They can't be defeated in a modern election unless the other side uses psych techniques, too. That's the main reason we've got a fighting chance. They've never had to use psych techniques in a situation where somebody's trying to neutralize their efforts. Anybody who can afford to use psych techniques against them is normally going to pull out and go someplace where he can manipulate people without any competition. I've seen a couple of things here that make it pretty clear Boyd's operation is set up on the assumption they only have to manipulate people who aren't being manipulated by a rival firm. It's their major weakness. We can't beat them if we don't take advantage of it."

"You've done everything you could to find some other alternative? You sat down with your backers and examined all the other possibilities you could think of and this is the only one that will work?"

"We examined the alternatives as thoroughly as you can examine any strategy without actually trying it. We have to use psych techniques if we're going to win. This may be our last chance to break up these organizations before they get so powerful nobody can break them up, and we won't stand a chance if we don't use the best strategy we've got. I didn't come here to ask you for minor help, Dr. Mead. We have to use psych techniques and we have to use them in support of the best candidate we can put in the field. Everything I've done so far indicates that you're the perfect candidate. Don't turn us down without giving this plenty of thought. The future of a hell of a lot of human beings could depend on your decision."

Mead started. The ice in his drink clinked against the side of the glass.

"You want me to be your front man?"

"You're the ideal candidate. Your age, your political views, your general philosophy—they all fit the requirements. And the fact that you've already had some political experience means it won't look like you just popped out of nowhere. We'll have to work like hell to get you nominated in the Republican primary, but if we can get you the nomination, you should win the general election, too."

"You want me to be the puppet in front of your computer, Dr. Nicholson? You want me to stand out there and wag my tongue the way your model tells me to?"

"You won't have to say one word you don't believe in. The main information I've gotten out of my model is a description of the kind of candidate who can win. The rest of the campaign will be as much like ordinary campaigning as I can make it. The major difference between the kind of campaign we'll run and the kind you might run anyway is the fact that you'll have experts giving you very precise advice about the kind of things you should say and when you should say them. Every candidate plays some of his beliefs down and emphasizes others. All I can do with my model is give you exact information about what you should be emphasizing at any given time."

Mead's scowl deepened. Nicholson's model of Mead's personality was still incomplete, but he had made some logical extrapolations from the data in his files, and he could visualize the pressures that were building up in Mead's psyche.

Mead had come of age in the late 1960's and he had been active in most of the political movements that had created a big stir around the time he had been in college. He had been a conscientious objector during the Indochina conflict and he had spent half of the 1970's in India, where he had lived on subsistence wages while he had worked with the volunteer team that had designed one of the biggest computerized educational systems in the world. And he had remained politically active until he had reached his middle forties; he had been a leader in an unsuccessful "reform Republican" organization only five years before, and he was still a leading figure in a couple of national political pressure groups, and an elder in a local Presbyterian church that was noted for its concern with social and political problems. He still made public statements now and then, and his latest statements indicated he still had strong feelings about cooperation and social responsibility. His commencement speech at the local state college had been a plea for more social responsibility and a long denunciation of the "hedonism, amorality and completely selfish individualism" which seemed to be the dominant characteristics of the present.

But people who were politically active tended to be politically ambitious, too. Mead had built up a first-rate computer firm when he had finally become a private businessman in his late thirties, and he tended to rise to the top every time he joined an organiza-

41

tion. Thousands of young men had worked in India and Africa during the seventies, but very few had written articles about it for national magazines. And fewer had ended up serving on the national board of the Foreign Policy Association. All of Nicholson's knowledge and experience told him there was a good chance he was dealing with a man who wanted power, status and fame, but who probably felt his hungers were basically evil—a personality type which had always been common in a country in which politicians were supposed to pretend they weren't motivated by the emotional needs that made people go into politics. Mead would never run for Congress merely because he had a healthy desire to be a United States congressman. He had to be convinced his election would serve some higher purpose. But he wanted to be convinced.

"I don't like using psych techniques any more than you do," Nicholson said. "I wasn't exaggerating when I said it took me six months to make up my mind to do this. I wouldn't ask you to help me do something like this if I didn't think it was unavoidable. Frankly, your political views and mine are so far apart I probably wouldn't even vote for you normally. But I knew I'd made the right decision the second time I came into this area and made a survey. Are you familiar with the development called Greenplace?"

"That old-fashioned place near Ashland, with all the trees? The one that looks like it hasn't changed in thirty years?"

"Right."

"What about it?"

"I made my second psych survey in June and ran into something nobody expected. I knew the cancers were powerful, but I didn't know how far they'd really gone. Boyd's people have arranged things so everybody in that development is the same Gruber type. I don't know exactly how they did it, but I've checked out my results twice now, and there's no doubt about it. They've managed to segregate a bunch of people into a nice compact little area where they can manipulate two thousand people as if they were dealing with one personality."

42

Mead's head jerked Nicholson had told seven different people about Greenplace during the last three months and none of them had looked as startled as Mead looked.

"They're doing that kind of thing to everybody who lives in Boyd's district," Nicholson said. "Every human being who lives in Windham County is being manipulated by some trick like that. And it's going to get worse in the future—and we won't have the slightest hope it's going to get better if we just sit back and wait. We've had political organizations like Boyd's all through our history, and sooner or later they've always fallen apart. Sooner or later the guy who founded them died and the organization collapsed, or somebody younger took it over and at least kept it in step with the times. But now we've got Martin Boyd sitting in Congress forty-eight years after the voters first sent him there, and he's got an artificial heart and a transplanted lung working in his chest, and an artificial gland strapped on his leg—and everybody who knows anything about medicine thinks were're only twenty years away from the day when people like Boyd will be able to buy themselves new bodies from the necks down. He's got the rest of eternity to play with and he isn't going to spend it dominating the people in one little congressional district. I know the guy who's handling Boyd's psych operations and I can almost guarantee you John Hill isn't going to stand still even if Boyd wants him to. If we don't do something about these cancers now, in another twenty years this whole country's going to be divided up into petty little baronies ruled by people like Boyd and their pet psych masters.

Mead's eyes dulled. He hid his big, round face behind his glass and sucked in a few drops of the drugs.

"I should have known they were doing things like that," Mead said. "I've watched those bastards operate for fifteen years. They'd skin their own children alive if they thought it would keep them in power."

"I checked the place out twice," Nicholson said. "I'd never thought about a gimmick like that before, but it isn't as difficult as it looks once you start thinking about it. There are a lot of ways you can attract a particular type of personality if you know what you're doing. You can pitch your ads that way; you can check out the people who apply and make sure you only let that type buy. You can't do it with everybody, but the models for some G-types are so good nowadays you can check out two or three important facts and deduce the rest of the personality from that. They can probably set up ads that are so good they can be sure eighty percent of the people who answer them are the type they want. And they can set up some relatively simple tests that can eliminate the other twenty percent after they get there. I didn't go into a lot of detail in that article in the *Times* but I wasn't exaggerating when I said you can type almost any human alive if you've got the resources. Any psychologist with a little ingenuity can take some of the tests we use in therapy nowadays and rearrange them so they can be used in real life situations."

"And you're willing to play tricks like that on people yourself? You're willing to set up a real life situation that will let you treat people like they're experimental animals who'll jump the way you want them when you turn on the right current?"

"It's the only way we can break them up," Nicholson said. "The only alternative that looks like it might be effective is a good old-fashioned assassination."

"Did you consider the possibility you might put some of your war chest into a couple of hours on TV and let people know what Boyd's doing to them? Have you people developed techniques that are so powerful the people in Greenplace would go on voting for Boyd after they knew he was doing that to them?"

"It won't work. I can't prove it won't work without sitting down in front of a computer with you for a couple of hours, but I can guarantee it won't work. There are some psych techniques you can neutralize by exposing them. But you can't tell a man a psych technique is manipulating emotion X if he can't even admit he feels emotion X. Most of the people who live in Greenplace probably think their neighborhood is as diversified as any neighborhood in the world. Half

44

of them probably don't even really believe you can type people."

Mead shook his head. He stared at the top of his drink and Nicholson waited while he thought.

"We're really living in a wonderful period," Mead said.

"Mmmmm."

"You're really pushing all the buttons, too. United States congressman. Power over other men's emotions. A good chance I could be a senator or a governor someday. And all for the best reasons in the world."

"All I'm offering you is a good chance that some psychological butcher may scramble up your personality. And a slight chance somebody may try to bash your head in, too."

"You don't think I'd like to beat Boyd just to get elected to Congress?"

"Enough to get mixed up in something like this? You might enjoy being a congressman, Dr. Mead, but I can't believe you've lost your hold on reality."

"And you're confident I won't be just as bad as Boyd if you manage to sell me to the voters. Your model can predict that, too?"

"Anybody we elect will be an improvement over Boyd. The new man may start using psych techniques on his own after he's elected. There's no way we can keep him from doing that. But you can't use psych techniques the way Boyd does unless you've got his kind of money behind you. Psych techniques are only part of the problem. The big danger is the combination: psych techniques in the hands of powerful, established organizations run by men who may be alive a hundred years from now."

"And you'll make sure I run into some opposition if it looks like I'm starting to build up the kind of organization Boyd has?"

Nicholson smiled. "Probably."

Mead smiled back. He hid behind his glass again and Nicholson settled back in his chair and sipped his drink.

"I have to admit you sound like you know what you're doing," Mead said. "I wouldn't think much of myself if I wasn't impressed by your courage, either. You're taking on a job that looks like it may be as dangerous as a full-scale war. I may not be able to go along with it myself, but I couldn't condemn you for it if I thought you were going to enjoy every dirty trick you're going to pull. I'll probably be very glad you did it if you manage to pull it off."

"The odds I'll pull it off will be a hell of a lot higher if you're willing to help us."

"There's nobody else in this whole county you can use for a front man?"

"The fact that you're already well known will probably make a significant difference when they start counting the votes. There may be other potential candidates around, but they'll be running under a handicap if they're complete newcomers to the political scene."

"And nobody in his right mind wants to go into something like this without the best equipment he can get."

"I don't think of you as equipment, Dr. Mead. I came to you first because I'd rather work with a human being instead of an actor who's just playing the role the computer tells him to play."

"I won't have to change my opinions to suit your model of the perfect candidate? I won't have to trim my hair a little here and there?"

"No more than a politician would normally. No more than you've probably done yourself when you wanted to get people to follow you."

"You can guarantee that?"

"You can tell me to go to Hell any time I ask you to do something you don't like. There's no way in the world I can make you do one damned thing you don't want to do."

"You can persuade a whole congressional district it should elect me to Congress and you can't persuade one man he should do something immoral?"

"We can't make them elect anybody we just happen to pull out of a hat. We can predict they'll elect a certain kind of man if he runs, and we can give them a candidate who fits the prescription—or who pretends he fits the prescription. But we can't work against

46

the voter's own desires. And the same limitation applies to individuals, too. We can't hypnotize you and lead you through this like a zombie."

"But you do have techniques for manipulating individuals, Dr. Nicholson. How do I know you haven't been giving me the kind of tests you've been talking about? How do I know you haven't been noting my reactions to everything you've said, so you can stick them in your model?"

Nicholson smiled. "I might have done that if I thought I could afford it. I don't have the resources to test every individual who might make a good candidate, however. And it isn't necessary, either. I had to look up your public record before I could predict you'd be a good candidate, but that's all I needed. And that doesn't give me fifty percent of the kind of information I'd need if I tried to build up a model of your personality. I can make some pretty shrewd guesses with the information I've got, but that's all I can do."

Mead studied Nicholson's face. "I'll be watching everything you do if I decide to do this. The first time I see any evidence you're manipulating me, that's it."

"I wouldn't want you to do anything else," Nicholson said. "You can watch us as carefully as you want to."

"How much time do I have before you have to have a definite answer?"

"I should have a definite answer in a couple of weeks. I'd like to give you all the time you feel you need, but I need time to look for an alternate if you don't think you can do it."

"You can give me a good look at the details of your plans? We can sit down in front of a computer and you can back up the kind of thing you've been telling me tonight?"

"I'll spend as much time with you as I possibly can."

"You aren't afraid I'll just pump you for information and then turn it over to Boyd?"

"It wouldn't make that much difference. We have to keep some of the details secret, but I'm planning our tactics on the assumption they'll know what our general strategy is and can probably work out the details, too. It's just like any other situation in which you use computer models in a conflict situation. There's plenty of room for maneuver but secrecy isn't that useful when the other side's got time to think."

"They probably could have predicted you'd come here and see me?"

"They've probably known you're a strong potential candidate for the last five years. They couldn't have predicted I'd come here first, but they probably knew you'd be on my list."

Mead shook his head. "You're beginning to make me feel like somebody should invent a time machine and eliminate Freud and Gruber."

"I'm just trying to be as honest as I can," Nicholson said. "It's a rough game and you shouldn't go into it with any illusions."

IV

NICHOLSON PULLED the stick out of his belt as he started down the path. Mead positioned himself on the porch with a loaded gas rifle in his hands.

"Elaine'll open the gate as soon as you get up to it," Mead said. "We'll leave it open till you're inside the taxi and on your way."

Nicholson trudged down the path with the stick hidden in his hand. The gate swung open in front of him and he checked the wall on each side and stepped through.

A big air cushion police car skimmed up to the landing. The door flew open. A big cop jumped out and planted himself between Nicholson and the taxi at the end of the landing.

Nicholson froze. He looked up at the eyes two inches above him and the big cop smiled down at him with the self-confidence of all the arrogant muscle men he had ever met.

"Stay right where you are, sonny. You've got a date with some people down at the station."

The cop in the car watched him with one hand on a grinning police dog. A blinking sign on the car warned him a camera was photographing everything he did.

Nicholson's body tensed. He glanced back at the house and saw Mead step off the porch.

He looked up at the smiling cop. "What's the problem, officer?"

"The chief wants a little talk with you. Climb in the car, laddy."

Footsteps hurried down the path. The cop in the car smiled.

"What's going on?" Mead said.

The cop in the car switched on his loudspeaker. "We've got three citizens at the courthouse who claim this man assaulted them with a deadly weapon. We're taking him in for questioning."

"That's ridiculous. I saw the whole thing. They attacked him."

The big cop smiled at the helpless bug in front of him. His hands swayed beside his jacket.

"Get in the car, sonny. Give daddy your little toy and come along."

Nicholson stared at the taxi rocking on the dark water. The cop was the only obstacle between him and the end of the landing. Two good blows with the stick and he could put the arrogant son of a bitch on the deck and reach the taxi before the other cop could move.

He had been afraid of the police station ever since he had started working on this project. If they ever got him inside that place and started working on him with drugs. . . .

The cop's hand moved slightly. The familiar, sour smell of a common anti-inhibitive gas surrounded Nicholson's face.

The stick leaped out. The big cop doubled over. Mead yelled.

A whistle shrieked. Another police car skimmed around Mead's island. A cop jumped on to the landing and crouched between Nicholson and the taxi with his hands raised. The dog and the other cop piled out of their car. Nicholson lunged with the stick extended like a sword and the cop in front of him laughed and jumped back.

Hands grabbed his shoulders. The dog snarled. He swung the stick at a laughing face and a hand chopped at his wrist and sent the stick flying.

V

MANY PEOPLE HAD still believed poverty could be abolished when Nicholson had been in his twenties. And in a sense they had been right. The people who had dreamed of eliminating poverty would have been dumbfounded if they had seen the home of a family which was living on the minimum income guaranteed by the United States government in the year 2000. The poorest man in the United States could now take his family to Europe every few years and could enjoy the kind of annual vacations middle class people had enjoyed in the 1960's. The children of lower income parents now studied in public schools that would have looked Utopian fifty years ago and came out of them with IQ's that were thirty points higher than they would have been if the children had attended the kind of schools Nicholson had attended. Every human being in America could eat as much food as his stomach could hold. Nobody ever had to complain about the nutritional value of the food he could afford.

The poor still existed, however. And many people were beginning to think they were going to be with us as long as the human race survived. The steady advance of technology had filled every American home with expensive consumer goods, but it had also created new forms of poverty. A wage earner who was supporting his family on sixteen thousand a year probably felt just as pinched and harassed as he would have felt if he had been living on four thousand a year in the 1960's. The goods that really counted in the modern world were out of his reach and he knew it.

In the middle of the twentieth century, lower income fathers had watched their daughters feel stunted and bitter because they couldn't buy them new dresses; in the first year of the twenty-first century, they had to watch their daughters eye middle class girls who looked like creatures out of daydreams because their parents could buy them medical cosmetic treatments that could remodel every inch of their bodies. The poorest family in the United States could take a trip to Europe, but the modern middle class citizen hopped to London for the weekend, went on shopping sprees in Africa and Asia and generally treated the planet Earth as if it were a good place to spend a weekend. Middle class children grew up with biochemical medical treatments and programmed educational toys that could add fifty or sixty points to their IQ's; middle class adults could buy "unnecessary" medical treatments that could keep them healthy and vigorous as long as they could stay alive.

And how did a lower income man feel when he watched a TV ad for a little item like continuous, lifelong psychotherapy? When he looked at a home in a neighborhood where you could step outside your house and breathe air that was just as pure as the filtered air in his bedroom? When he heard about expensive custom-made learning programs that could teach you how to really enjoy friendship and family life?

Wakefield Castles was a perfect symbol of the plight of the lower income family. There were hundreds of developments just like it all over the country, and they were mentioned in every study of the problems of the poor. The five-story houses in the development were crowded with luxuries that would have astonished any aristocrat who had lived before 1900. Every basement contained a swimming pool. Elevators connected the different floors. Aerial pictures of the development always showed yards cluttered with luxurious toys and expensive pets.

The houses themselves were only fifteen feet square, however. And each house sat on a lot that was only fifty feet square. Thirty-five thousand families lived in a square two miles on a side, each identical, prefabricated house surrounded by a white plastic wall that made the development look like a checkerboard covered with walled castles. Thirty-five thousand families filled their homes with luxuries and stared out of their windows at a landscape that told them they were too poor to buy the things that were really scarce and valuable. The automated factories could mass-produce gadgets but they couldn't mass-produce land, and one hundred and fifty million people now lived in the eastern megalopolis between Washington and Boston. On an income of sixteen thousand a year, you couldn't even afford a one bedroom apartment in the kind of interesting, conveniently located neighborhood Nicholson lived in. All you could afford on that kind of income was a fifty-foot lot in a crowded "surburban" development that had been set down in the middle of nowhere.

The police car turned off the main road and entered the development twenty minutes after it left Mead's house. The entire development had been built on a huge plastic slab and the car raced across it through the system of tunnels that had been built into the slab.

Smooth white walls flashed by the car two inches from its side. The driver turned into another tunnel a good half mile inside the development and the car stopped in front of a section of the wall labeled 2621. The wall slid open and the driver eased them through the opening and parked in a garage that was about three feet wider than the car.

The wall hissed shut. The big cop jerked the scrambler he had been pointing at Nicholson's face. "We've got two of these little gadgets and we've got the dog. You're down here in the middle of nowhere and you aren't going to go far if you try to make a run for it. Do what we tell you without giving us any trouble and you may come out of this in better shape than you think."

The driver turned around and stuck a plastic card in the lock that was holding Nicholson's handcuffs against the ceiling. The lock clicked open and Nicholson lowered his arms.

The two cops pushed open the front doors and backed out of the car. They lined up along the driver's side with their scramblers aimed at the back door.

"Open the door and step outside. Don't move too fast."

The dog watched Nicholson from the other end of the back seat. He turned away from it with his back cringing and reached for the handle.

He pushed the door open and eased himself out. An elevator slid open and the driver stopped the door with his body.

"Harry gets in first. Then you. Then the dog. Stand in the middle of the elevator when you get inside and face the back."

The big cop backed into the elevator with the scrambler trained on Nicholson's face. Nicholson followed him in and the dog jumped out of the car and trotted across the plastic floor as soon as the driver called it. The cops took up positions in the front of the elevator and the driver reached out and pushed a button.

A whiff of chlorine sneaked through the door as the elevator rose past the swimming pool. The driver leaned against the side of the elevator and eyed Nicholson's face as if he was looking at a specimen in the zoo.

"He's one of the silent ones," the big cop said.

The elevator stopped at the third floor. The door opened and the driver jerked his head.

The room looked like it took up the entire third floor. A life-size TV screen filled the wall on his right and most of the other furniture looked like it belonged in a den. The only door in the place looked like it probably opened on a balcony. The only window was a shoulder high slit that extended along most of the outside wall.

The elevator door closed behind him. The lights blinked out. He jumped back and raised his hands.

He lowered his hands and blinked hard. The stolid, expressionless mask he had worn in the car settled over his face. His eyes adjusted to the dark and he edged up to the door and made sure it was locked.

He picked his way across the room and hit the window with the edge of his handcuffs. The impact vibrated through his arm bones and he inched across the room and groped along a set of bookshelves.

His hands closed around a metal bust he had noticed when he had stepped out of the elevator. He raised it above his head with both hands and threw it at the window. It thunked against the burglarproof glass and he paused in the middle of the room and stared out the window at the lights of the other towers that sprawled across the landscape.

He sat down in one of the armchairs and crossed his legs as if he was posing for an ad for a happy drink. Brahm's Lullaby hummed in his mind, the same music he had used to calm himself when he had gotten panicky before a test while he had been going to graduate school.

Color spread across the big TV screen. A round-faced, boyish young man smiled at him from behind a desk.

"Good evening, Dr. Nicholson. How are you tonight?"

Nicholson turned around in the chair and stared at the screen without changing his expression. He had never met John Hill before but he knew him as soon as he saw him.

"It's a real pleasure to meet you," Hill said. "I've been reading your column in *Current Psychology* ever since you first started writing it and I studied some of your earlier stuff when I was in graduate school, too. It's a real honor to meet a man with your reputation in our field."

Nicholson stared at the screen without answering. Everybody who knew John Hill said he was the kind of man who still said sir and ma'am to his elders, made nice mouth noises at old ladies and generally did all the polite, thoughtful things his parents had told him he should do when he had been growing up in South Carolina. He had gone to work for a large political organization two weeks after he had received his Ph.D. in psychology, but his mother had never told him there might be something wrong with that.

"I hope our friends on the police force didn't get disrespectful, Dr. Nicholson. I told them not to use any more force than they had to, but I'm afraid it's hard to control the kind of people we get for police nowadays when you aren't right there on the spot. And I'm afraid I had a lot of work to do here in Washington and couldn't get away."

Nicholson stared at the screen with a face made out of stone. His eyes started to drift toward the metal bust on the floor and he locked them on the screen and held them there.

"Please go right ahead and react, Dr. Nicholson. You may as well be comfortable. Any information we get out of the way you react isn't going to make our model of you any more accurate than it already is. We've been using all the standard surveillance techniques for the last six weeks, and we gave you a few field tests you may not have noticed, too. And I think the results of our work tonight prove we've come up with an accurate model."

He would probably hear the elevator when it started up the shaft. He might even gain something useful if he threw the bust at the phone. Hill would run into problems if he was planning an automated operation and his cameras broke.

Hill folded his hands on his desk. "I'm certain you already realize we knew how you'd be feeling when the policeman flipped the anti-inhibitive gas at you. You've probably guessed we set up that little fight you had earlier in the evening, too. I set that up on the basis of a conjecture, of course, based on the fact that your records indicated you'd never actually engaged in violence. But I think it shows you just how subtly we can lead you around when we put our minds to it. I hope you appreciate the fact that I set this up so it began with something you probably enjoyed."

The round face smiled again. Nicholson stared back at it and Hill lowered his head and studied a paper on his desk.

"As you undoubtedly know, Dr. Nicholson, you are primarily a Gruber type G-6, a superego type in the language of the popularizers. I would have been extremely surprised if you'd fitted into any other pattern, considering your background, but I think you'll be pleased to know that one of the findings of our speciality has been confirmed once again. It's one of the closest fits I've ever seen, in fact. Seventy-five percent of the information we've collected fits the latest standard model. Less than two percent conflicts with it."

Nicholson swallowed. His eyes wavered again and he swung them back to Hill's face and stared at it as if he was trying to hypnotize him.

"I'm still surprised you did something like this. It's the kind of thing G-6's tend to do, but we've got quite a few of them in our congressional district and most of them seem to be satisfied helping the sick or working with political groups in which they don't have to worry about the kind of unpleasant experience you're going through now. I've even tried to set things up so they can win little merit badges and join organizations that are trying to make the world a better place to live. I can't believe you honestly thought you could come over here as often as you have and not have us lead you into a trap, Dr. Nicholson. Or have you reached the point where your need to live up to whatever ideal you're trying to live up to has become more important than anything that can happen to you?"

One, two, three, four, five, six, seven, eight, nine . . .

"I'm afraid I've never really understood G-6's myself. It's always looked to me like that particular personality structure should be such a burden you'd have it modified as soon as you could afford it. Or is that kind of self-sacrifice part of the self-image you're trying to build up?"

Forty-one. Forty-two. Forty-three. Forty-four.

"Our model predicted you would just sit here like this, by the way. It looks extremely uncomfortable under the circumstances, but you may as well do whatever you feel like doing. I don't want to sound crude, but it really doesn't matter what you do."

Seventy-five. Seventy-six. Seventy-seven.

"We've set up this meeting because we want you to help us with a project. We've decided that the best way to keep you from disrupting our operations is to take advantage of the fact that married G-6's generally have a strong sense of loyalty to their families. We're going to arrange things so a member of your family will be a kind of hostage, a procedure that should be much more effective than a threat to yourself. We went to a lot of trouble and expense getting you modeled, however, and I'm afraid I've been told I have to watch my budget. In a few minutes the policemen are going to return to this room and talk you into answering a few questions we have here. The techniques they're going to use will probably seem crude to you, considering the era we're living in. Tomorrow, however, there will be no drugs in your bloodstream. There will be no evidence anyone has tampered with your personality. It will be a simple case of ordinary police brutality. The kind of thing cops do all the time when somebody strikes a member of the force with a deadly weapon. Two of the policemen will even be reprimanded and suspended from the force."

The screen blurred. Nicholson rose out of the chair before he could stop himself.

"I think you can imagine the kind of things an organization like ours can do when we get an adequate model of a personality. You got a good demonstration tonight and that was relatively unimaginative. I don't know exactly what we'll be able to do when we get your wife adequately typed, but I'm certain you can think of the possibilities as well as I can. The things we can put in her mail, the phone calls we can make, the techniques we can use to lead her into accidents . . . crimes . . . adulteries. . . . And we don't even have to spend a lot of time and money investigating her. We can get everything we need to know from a man who's been observing her private life since 1989."

The handcuffs bit into Nicholson's wrists. He raised them above his head and Hill stared at him over his folded hands and watched him step toward the screen.

"You son of a bitch. You sadistic little cancer."

Equipment echoed in the elevator shaft. Hill glanced at the papers on his desk.

"We need the answers to the following questions, Dr.

Nicholson. One—who picked the names of your daughters, you or Susan? Two—how many times per week do you and Susan have sexual intercourse? Has there been a change in the frequency since you were married? If yes, please chart the rise and fall. Three—"

Nicholson swung away from the screen. He dropped to his knees beside the window and stood up with the bust between his hands.

"What did your parents think of your marriage? Four—which of your daughters does Susan like the most? The least? Five—"

Nicholson scurried across the room and took up a position beside the elevator. The door slid open and he raised the bust above his head with both hands.

VI

NICHOLSON HAD BEEN haunted by Susan Light for more than four weeks before he had asked her for a date. He had played around with her crowd at three different street festivals and he had known she would be a dangerous girl to get involved with if you knew you weren't going to be satisfied with the knowledge you had bedded her once or twice. She had been a beautiful, wild-haired girl who had been making twice as much money as he had been making then, and she had been at the center of a crowd every time he had seen her. It had been months since she had spent an evening at home. Everybody who had known her had told him she prowled through young men the way men had always hunted women, bedding this one because she liked his looks, that one because he was good at sex, another one because he appealed to some emotional need, or because his desire flattered her. Girls had still tended to claim they were looking for "meaningful relationships" in those days, but Sue had been more like the completely free, completely amoral girl you met nowadays. Her mother had sprinkled her sex education with slogans like "Sex is supposed to be shared and enjoyed, not used," but Sue had left that kind of piety behind her before she had left her teens. Daddy had given her presents when she had smiled at him, and she could see no reason why the young men she knew couldn't give her pleasure, attention, and everything else she wanted in return for whatever she was giving them. Sue's mother had thought she was being very bold when she had told her elders God was dead; she had been very upset when Sue had finished the quotation by agreeing with Ivan Karamazov and concluding that everything was therefore permitted.

Nicholson had been a fashionable young dandy who had bedded some of the most attractive young girls in the city, but he had been as nervous as a schoolboy the first time he had bedded Susan. She had been as generous as any girl he had ever known, but the other men who had enjoyed her had hovered in the back of his mind, as if she had been judging a contest and their scores had all been marked on a chart. Most of the men who had bedded her had been lucky if they had spent two nights with her before she had drifted away from them. How long would he last if he couldn't please her as much as they had?

There had been times during the next three years when he had stood in the middle of his apartment and cursed the emotions that made him want a girl like Susan Light. Sometimes he would run into her at a street carnival and see her laughing with somebody who was obviously looking forward to the rest of the evening. Sometimes he would call her up for a date and she would be jetting off to Africa or Europe for a weekend jaunt with some of her friends. He could dance and play and sex as well as anybody she knew, but that was no guarantee you could succeed when you were after the one thing she had never given anybody. He wanted her to love him and marry him, not party with him. And that was the one thing she wasn't going to give anybody until she was damn well ready.

He had adopted the only strategy that could possibly work with a girl like her and he had held on to it as if he had been holding on to a rope on the side of a mountain. He had assumed she would probably want to get married sooner or later and he had made sure he would still be on her list of eligible men when the time came. He had pushed his career and become one of the most financially successful young psychologists in the region; he had enjoyed three very fine love affairs and bedded several other girls who had been as attractive as Sue would ever be; and he had traveled around the planet and put on exceptional parties and generally established himself as somebody who would make a pretty impressive husband. He had assumed normal women tended to pick men who looked stable and dependable when they started hunting for husbands —and he had been certain nobody looked sillier than a man who was constantly dancing attendance on a woman who wasn't ready for him.

It had taken every ounce of self-control he possessed, but he had been driven by the emotion that had dominated everything he had ever tried. And in the end, he had pushed himself forward at a moment that could have been selected by a computer and grabbed the dream he had been stalking for three years.

A sharp-eyed judge watched Ralph Nicholson everywhere he went. It had been watching him ever since he had been a child and it was probably going to be watching him as long as he lived. It had been watching him all through the years he had been weaving a net around Sue and it had been watching him when he had realized psychotherapy and self-knowledge were challenges that frightened him more than any challenge he had ever encountered. It had gravely nodded approval when young Ralph Nicholson had given some of the best parties his friends had ever seen. It had patted him on the head and smiled benignly every time young Ralph Nicholson had walked out of his apartment and gone into the streets of the city dressed in the latest fashions and skilled at singing, dancing, lovemaking, and all the other trades a young man had to know in a world in which leisure had become a more important arena than work. His personality was a mixture of all the emotions and drives that make up a human being, but the forces that mold personalities had shaped it into the structure Gruber's research teams had put in Group Six: a personality dominated by a tremendous need to maintain its self-esteem and live up to some kind of ideal self-image. Every time Ralph Nicholson made a move, the judge in his skull watched and measured.

The pages of *The Journal of Theoretical Psychology* were loaded with carefully reasoned arguments about the factors that produced that kind of personality. Psychologists tended to be fascinated by it; thirty-seven percent of the psychotherapists in the United States were G-6's. Some theorists thought the main factors were emotional deprivation and a general assault on the ego during the first three years of life; G-6's would cease to trouble the human species, according to this view, if parents would merely fondle their infants and give them plenty of emotional support. Other theorists thought the primary causes could be found in the family patterns of many middle class American homes. If a young boy didn't see his father enough, the argument ran, he got his picture of normal male behavior out of books and the mass media and tended to grow up with an exaggerated image of normal manhood; a tragic victim of the illusion men really are fearless and resourceful and always right. Others theorized about the effects of genes, accidents of physical development and the different ways individuals could respond to the general culture. Most of these factors could be found in the history of any American male who could be classified as a G-6.

Most of these ideas were only interesting speculations, however. To a modern, computer-oriented therapist, the human personality was a system which was shaped by the interaction of hundreds of factors; thousands of different mixtures could produce the same basic personality structure. Occasionally, with a little luck, a researcher could prove that certain factors had produced a certain individual. But most of the time you could only draw a chart of the finished structure and put it in a classification and use the chart to make predictions about its future behavior.

Ralph Nicholson was a Gruber type G-6 and he was

probably going to be a Gruber type G-6 as long as he lived. He had learned to live with the son of a bitch who watched him but he could never eliminate him completely. He could have gone to one of his colleagues and submitted to one of the techniques that drastically modified the personality, but in the end he would only have been different; there was no guarantee he would be better or happier. There was no such thing as the ideal personality. Every set of drives had its pleasures and its pains and you only modified them when they were so painful or crippling you couldn't live with them.

Every personality had its weaknesses. Every human hunger could be turned against you once the manipulators knew it was there. Every human personality had its breaking point. How many men his age could have resisted them when they had kicked him in the stomach and he had felt himself throwing up for the third time? How long could any normal human being take it when they were hitting you in the head and you knew they were making little pinpoint hemorrhages in your brain every time they hit you?

Everybody cracked sooner or later. Nobody could lie there and take it forever. How many psychologists had been sitting in their houses while he had been running around the world trying to do something about the problems their science had created?

"I'll have to talk to John and Abe before I can tell you anything definite," the young lawyer said. "But right now it looks to me like our best bet is the police brutality charge. We'll probably bring a suit in federal court and use that to bargain with the cancers. It might get expensive but right now it looks to me like there's probably a good chance we can get you off with a suspended sentence. We'll have trouble proving they didn't take you directly to the police station—the whole police force will swear they did that—but it looks like it's pretty damned obvious they didn't have to rough you up like that just to keep you from attacking them. It's hard to get around the fact that you actually hit one of the cops but they damned sure didn't need to do that to you."

The gray New Jersey landscape drifted across Nicholson's consciousness. A TV truck swooshed by on the right and slowed down in front of them. The turret swung around and aimed a camera at the notorious Dr. Nicholson and the young lawyer who was driving him back to Philadelphia.

"That's the only thing that really bothers me," the lawyer said. "I hope that kind of publicity won't have a bad effect on your practice."

"It's hard to say," Nicholson said.

"I guess you don't have any shortage of customers in your profession."

"That's usually the least of our worries."

"You don't think they did it because of those articles you've been writing, do you? Abe told me he thought Boyd's gang had it in for you."

"I've been doing some research for a documentary."

"On the Boyd organization?"

"Right."

"We can probably sue them for violating your civil rights if there's any evidence that's involved in it. We could have a pretty big chip to bargain with if we could threaten them with an accusation that all the unnecessary force was part of an attempt to interfere with the freedom of the press. The courts are getting pretty strict about unnecessary force these days. They might even give us damages for that at the same time they're upholding a conviction for assaulting a police officer."

A big, freckle-faced girl met them in the lobby of the main hospital complex and led them to a private emergency room on the second floor. The lawyer sat down in an armchair with his notebook in his hand and the medical team trooped in. Technicians stuck needles in Nicholson's body and took samples of his blood. A camera photographed his eyes under different types of lighting. Busy hands scurried across his body with machines and medicines and removed every trace of the beating except the patch they strapped over his left eye.

"You'll probably be pretty close to normal by tomorrow," the chief physician said. "They gave you a lot of cuts and bruises but they didn't damage any internal organs. I'd like to see the cancers spend the next ten years in jail but I have to admit I've seen them work people over worse than this."

Most of the people in the lobby eyed him curiously when he came down the stairs. A newsman pointed another TV camera at him. Ellen smiled her "There's daddy" smile and jumped out of the chair she had been squirming in. Sue stood up and he walked toward her with his eyes locked on her face.

"I've got a cab waiting outside," Sue said. "I tried to time it so we'd get here just before they said you'd be ready."

He squeezed her shoulder and nodded. The girls gathered up their female baggage and they hurried toward the door with the cancer with the TV camera scuttling along beside them. The cab pulled away from the curb as soon as he stuck his credit card in the slot and he settled back in his seat and made himself smile wryly.

"I hope I look dashing with an eye patch."

Nancy cocked her head and stared at him quizzically. "Are you going to wear it forever, daddy."

"It's just for a day. It's just to keep me from getting germs in my eye while it's healing."

"What kind of a man tried to attack you?"

"It was just some young hoodlums."

"Mommy really was worried. She didn't go to bed all night."

"I called Bob at midnight," Sue said. "He got Abe on the phone right away and Peggy Dazella and some of the people in her dojo gang started looking for you. I would've been there this morning if they hadn't told me you didn't want me there."

"I didn't want you to see me before the doctors cleaned me up a little."

"It was the worst night I've spent since we got married."

He reached across the taxi and patted her knee. She squeezed his hand and he looked down at Ellen and rumpled her hair with his other hand.

"Have you had any lunch yet?" Sue asked.

"I didn't even have breakfast. They offered me some

at the police station but I was afraid it would interfere with the blood tests."

"You went to a police station?" Nancy said.

"I had to tell them what happened."

Sue pulled her phone out of her purse and gave
their computer a group of numbers that sounded like
the codes for soup and a good selection of easily di-
gestible foods. She put the phone back in her purse
and Nicholson lowered his eyes and rumpled the top
of Lorin's hair.

He left the table as soon as they finished lunch and
trudged back to the bedroom. The tranquilizers were
still sitting on the shelf but he dropped down on the
bed without touching them.

He gave the computer an order and the big entertainment screen at the foot of the bed lit up. The reso-
nant, measured sound of one of Haydn's *Divertimenti
for Baryton, Cello, and Violin* filled the room. Gold
and gray mist moved across the screen as if he was
staring at Prince Esterhazy's fireplace and the prince
and his musicians were playing behind him.

A red light glowed under the phone screen. Sue
padded down the hall. The door opened and he fixed
his eyes on the deep, shifting fog on the screen.

"Bob Dazella's on the phone, honey. Do you think
you can talk to him?"

"Can you tell him he can call me in the morning?
At the office."

"He sounds like he really wants to see you."

"Tell him I said he already knows everything important. I'll fill in the details in the morning but they
aren't significant. I've got a critical appointment tomorrow morning and the doctor told me I should get all
the rest I can get."

"What about Ed Saboletsky? He says Ed wants to
talk to you, too."

"I'll talk to him later, too."

"You're going to be in here all day?"

"I can't miss this appointment tomorrow. They told
me to get all the rest I could get and this is the last
chance I'm going to get."

The door slid shut. Gold and gray swirled across the

screen as if he was moving through a fog that grew thicker and thicker as he moved through it.

We have your wife for a hostage, Dr. Nicholson. We wanted that and I meant it when I said we'll use it if we have to. Please don't think I'm bluffing when I said that. But I think you understand that's only part of this. You've betrayed your wife, Dr. Nicholson, and you did it because you couldn't take a little pain. We didn't even have to use sophisticated torture techniques. We gave you a beating that would have looked mild to most of the people who've been beaten and tortured in the history of the world. And you screamed for mercy and handed us your wife in a nice, neatly wrapped package.

Saboletsky would know what they had to do twenty minutes after they started questioning him under drugs. They would lead him down the halls to the inpatient psychiatric pavilion and the therapy of choice would begin. His emotions would be numbed with drugs and he would be introduced to carefully chosen role players who had been told about his terrible crime. The role players would shake hands and say hello—they would probably tell him it was an honor to meet such a distinguished member of their profession—and he would be taken away and left in the company of people who would treat him like an honored guest. Every day he would spend a few more minutes with the people who knew he had betrayed his wife. Every day he would tell them a little more about his failure. Little by little their emotions would teach him his betrayal wasn't as disgusting as his emotions said it was.

No simple insight into himself could help him. He understood himself as well as any human could and he was still paralyzed. They had taken the very emotion that had driven him into Windham County and turned it against him. They had zeroed in on the girder that kept the whole structure standing and they had pushed it out of place with the precise force that would weaken the entire structure. Anything could be turned against you if the cancers knew you well enough. Nobody could stand up to an organization like Boyd's.

Only a fool would try to challenge them.

Sue padded down the hall again. The red light on the phone was still glowing.

"He says he's really anxious, honey. He says Ed thinks he should talk to you right away."

Muscles tensed all over Nicholson's body. He focused his eyes on the screen and hid his emotions behind a frown.

"Tell him I said I'll see him first thing tomorrow. I couldn't talk to him now if they pumped me full of energizers."

He looked up and saw her frown. "I really am tired," he said. "I'll be all right tomorrow, but right now I feel like curling up in a ball and sleeping for the next week."

The door slid shut. The gray and gold fog swirled in front of him.

He looked down at his watch and set the alarm before he forgot. Tomorrow morning he would wake up fifteen minutes before Sue usually woke up. He would stay awake tonight until he was certain she was sleeping.

VII

Ed Saboletsky stared at him from the phone screen. The sour smell of anti-inhibitive gas surrounded his chair. His head rolled drunkenly.

"They've got me in a cage, Ed. They worked me over and I told them everything they needed to get Sue modeled. They've got her at their mercy and I'm the cancer that set her up for it. They didn't use anything on me except their fists. And I broke down and gave them my own wife. I betrayed my own wife."

Fists hammered at his stomach. Nausea spread across his chest and throat. A hard hand slapped his face. "I'll repeat the questions once again, Dr. Nicholson. One—"

"Dr. Robert Dazella is calling from Washington, D.C."

Nicholson slumped back in his chair and stared at the big phone screen on the front wall of his office. The nozzle with the anti-inhibitive gas pointed at his face from the left side of his console.

67

"Accept the call."

The phone screen lit up. Dazella scowled at him across the office.

"I should have known you'd really be sitting beside that damned console," Dazella said. "Hasn't anybody ever told you the only guys that go to work the day after they've been beaten up are the guys that live in TV land?"

Nicholson squinted at the screen through his unbandaged eye. His screwed up face hid his emotions better than the disciplined mask he put on when he was dealing with patients.

"I've got a critical appointment at ten o'clock. I'm still a little sore but they didn't do anything serious."

"That was very kind of them. How the hell did they ever con you into hitting a cop in the middle of Boyd's own territory?"

Nicholson's eye drifted away from the screen. The nozzle pointed at him like a finger.

"They hit me with an a-h gas. It doesn't show up in the films but the cop had a gas projector hidden in his hand. He told me he was taking me in for questioning about the fight I had when I was going into Mead's and then he sprayed me with the gas."

"And he knew you'd hit him if he did that? How'd they know you wouldn't kiss the son of a bitch?"

They've been studying me for weeks. They ran the rat through the maze and studied the results until they found the stress that would make him stay off their turf. Talk to Saboletsky. Ask Saboletsky what happens when you make a Gruber type G-6 do something so disgusting he chokes when he tries to—

Nicholson shrugged. "They've probably got me all mapped out in their computer just like we thought they would. They could have made an educated guess and assumed anybody who's trying to unseat a political authority figure would probably hate cops, too. But I'll be pretty damned surprised if they don't have me modeled."

"I feel pretty damned surprised you're still able to sit up and talk. How did your talk with Mead go?"

"He wants to think about it for awhile. He's inter-

68

ested but he isn't sure he can work with people who dirty their hands with psych techniques."

"What does he want us to do—appeal to reason?"

"He thinks you can eliminate psych techniques by telling the voters what their glorious leaders are doing to them. I tried to tell him it wouldn't work but he still wants to think about it."

"And you think you can actually convince him he should put his scruples in the closet for awhile?"

"I have a feeling his opinion about the morality of it will probably be determined by how much he wants to be a congressman."

"I hope he makes up his mind before it's too late to file for the Goddamned primary. Have you talked to Saboletsky yet?"

Nicholson's muscles tensed. He locked his eye on the screen and squinted a little harder.

"He'll probably call me sometime today."

"You'd better let him take a look at you right away. I don't like to sound like a damned mother hen, Ralph, but I won't really believe they set this thing up just so they could beat you up until Ed's given you a complete checkup. I can't believe they'd go to all that trouble and then have a couple of guys work you over. Are you sure the people at the hospital gave you a thorough check for drugs?"

"They checked everything they could possibly check."

"It doesn't make sense. They've got the assault and battery charge they can hold over you but I'll be damned if I can believe they'd go to all this trouble just for that, either. They can harass you with court calls but I talked to Abe yesterday and he said he thinks there's a good chance he can get this whole thing settled in a couple of months and get you off with a fine or a short suspended sentence. People like Boyd don't pull their punches when they go after somebody. They point themselves right at the jugular vein and they don't move until they're sure they're going to sink their teeth in it."

Nicholson smiled wryly. "Maybe they thought they'd try something cheap first. Boyd likes to keep government spending down."

"The only money that son of a bitch worries about is money that won't buy him votes. I'm not going to feel right about this until Saboletsky gives you a thorough checkout and makes sure Hill didn't have them slip in a little psychology while you thought they were just beating you up."

"I'll call Saboletsky as soon as I get a chance."

"Today?"

"I'll get over there today or tomorrow. Don't worry about it."

"I'll worry about it until he gives you the cleanest bill of health I ever saw. You may not be the smartest friend I've ever had but life would be a hell of a lot duller if somebody ever psyched you into having any sense."

Nicholson stared at the blank screen after he signed off. Anguish twisted his face. His hand hovered over the a-h nozzle like a claw.

How many times do you and Susan have sexual intercourse per week?

... Once ... or ... twice. ...

Who named your first daughter, you or Susan?

... She. ...

Who?

Her! Sue! My wife!

Did you approve?

You son of a bitch.

Did you approve?

. . . .

Did you approve?

"Miss Julia Keenan is here for her appointment."

"Send her in."

The door slid open. A slender blonde woman stepped into the office.

Emotional reflexes took over. He stood up and smiled his friendliest smile. He was still a therapist and Julia Keenan needed him as much as she would need any human being she would ever meet. Her tests had indicated she would need a type of therapy that would take several hours, and Thursday was the only weekday she would be free all day. And you didn't give a woman an extra week to change her mind when she was struggling with the kind of problem Julia Keenan was struggling with. She was lucky she had managed to come to a therapist in the first place.

She smiled back as she walked across the room. Her hips swayed pleasantly.

"I hope I didn't make you get out of bed before you should have, Dr. Nicholson. I started to call you up and tell you we could reschedule your appointment, but I decided you'd probably call me up if you couldn't make it."

"The only thing that's still bothering me is this silly eye patch. I'd be perfectly normal if it weren't for that and it's coming off tomorrow."

"I saw some of the incident on the news. It looked to me like it was one of the most inexcusable things I've seen the police do yet."

"I hope this squint doesn't look too terrifying."

"I think it looks rather dashing."

She kept her back straight as she sat down. She glanced at the computer printouts on the console and smiled brightly.

"How did I do? Do I get the long treatment or the short one?"

He leaned back in his chair and tried to look relaxed. "It looks like you get the short one. It looks like there's a good chance we can get the whole problem cleared up in time for a late lunch, in fact."

He waited while she recovered from the first shock. Women with her problem always looked stunned when they heard the news. She had known that women with her problem could be divided into three types, but she had made the same assumption her type always made; she had assumed she was the type that was afraid of sex or the type that had trouble making commitments. She had come to the office prepared to undergo deconditioning therapy which would weaken her fear of sex, or long-term learning therapy which would strengthen her ability to make commitments—and the therapist was telling her he was going to give her three hours of intensive, classic Freudian psychoanalysis instead.

"I've got everything set up and ready to go," Nicholson said. "I can give you a relaxer right away, and after that it will be completely out of your hands. You'll be completely numb emotionally. It's as painless as an operation."

She stared at the printouts. She was an intelligent woman who had been exposed to plenty of first class science writing and she understood the situation; she knew the treatment was supposed to give her a new insight into her personality and she knew what the insight would be. Insight therapy only helped women with her problem when the computer predicted the client had idealized her father because she had been repressing an intense hatred for him. The treatment he was offering her would bring that hatred to the surface, and that single piece of self-knowledge would change her behavior as soon as she integrated it into her personality. The idealized father figure would be shattered and she would no longer be dominated by the feeling marriage was an attack on her father. She would stop having love affairs with men she couldn't marry and she would start making a realistic attempt to find a husband.

"The prognosis for this type of therapy is now ninety-five percent in cases like yours," Nicholson said. "There's nothing to it once you take the first drug. All I need is your permission."

"It doesn't make sense. I've been friends with my father since I was a baby. We haven't had a quarrel since I was a teenager."

"I ran your tests through the computer three times. There's only one more test I can make. If the diagnosis is wrong, you won't come out of the therapy with the insight most people get. You'll be one of the five percent we still make errors on and we'll start with one of the other therapies."

"You have to start with this one? You have to put me through that first?"

"The other therapies cost three times as much and they usually take four or five weeks. And they won't give you any help at all if the diagnosis is correct."

"And what if you try one of them first and it works? I don't want to argue with you, Dr. Nicholson, but I can't stand that Freudian insight stuff. I just want to change a stupid behavior pattern. I can't stand people who are always contemplating their little psyches and telling you why everybody does this and that."

"This is the only way we can change your behavior pattern if the diagnosis is correct, Miss Keenan. It will change it almost overnight—and nothing else will."

Her right hand gripped the arm of her chair. She stared at the console as if she was totally bewildered and he tried not to watch her like a hunter. He couldn't be detached. He wanted her to make the choice that would make her happy.

"I can't give you a sales talk, Miss Keenan. I'm not here to persuade you. I can tell you the best course of action you can take according to the knowledge we have at present, but I can't try to convince you that you should take it. We gave you tests that have been used thousands of times during the last ten years and we matched them against personality patterns that have been checked and rechecked for two decades now. And everything we've done indicates this is the best place to start. You may belong to the five percent but we can't know it and go on to something else until you've tried this. I can try one of the other therapies if you insist but it will probably be a tremendous waste of time and money."

"It's like asking me to believe black is white. I know it's supposed to be an unconscious emotion but that doesn't make it any more believable. I can't believe something like that can be true."

"You don't have to believe it," Nicholson said. "You just have to agree to undergo therapy and see what happens. It's an experiment. If the theory's wrong, it won't work."

Some of his colleagues would have turned the gas on her and started the therapy whether she wanted it or not; the entire process would be painless as soon as the first drug started working on her mind, and they could guarantee she would be glad they had done it when it was over. They were liberating her from her crippling emotions. She couldn't make a rational decision until after she had been given the treatment.

People like Nicholson were abdicating their responsibility when they offered a client treatment and the client had to "choose" it for himself.

He had never violated his principles, however, and he hoped he never would. Clients had left him just as crippled as they had come in and he had let them go. He didn't want to live in a world in which a therapist could "treat" anybody who "needed" treatment. His rules might not make sense when you applied them to a particular case, but they were one more flimsy barrier against a social milieu in which he and his colleagues could alter people whenever they thought it would be good for them.

She chuckled nervously. "Does this prove you're right? That I'm resisting like this?"

"I can't tell you. It might influence your decision."

"And you can't influence my decision?"

"I'm trying to be as objective as possible. I'm trying to present this so it will have the minimum effect on your emotions."

"What happens afterward? What happens when I go home and I don't have the drugs?"

"That's the part that sometimes gets very painful. We can numb your emotions during the actual therapy but you still have to adjust to your new insight into yourself afterward. I'll give you a prescription you can use when it gets bad and I'll give you some post-therapeutic guidance after you leave the treatment room. You can call me any time you feel like you need to talk. The computer will fill in for me if I'm busy or you'll be immediately referred to a specialist in that phase of the process if the computer can't help you. I've never had a case like yours last more than a couple of weeks, Miss Keenan. With the drugs and the other help we can give you nowadays, even the post-therapeutic phase is usually relatively mild most of the time. We've got a whole arsenal of techniques we can use once we know how you're reacting to it."

"And it won't work if the diagnosis isn't correct? I won't come out of the treatment believing something that isn't true?"

"The drugs we give you lower your resistance to

self-knowledge. They make it easier to think about frightening emotions and they speed up your thinking processes. Nothing we're going to give you will make you more suggestible."

She settled back in her chair. Her hands twitched nervously. She stared at him across the console and he shut up and waited.

"You can put me under as soon as I tell you?"

"Immediately."

"Go. Now. Hurry."

He twisted a nozzle on the console. A fine mist covered her face. The sudden touch of the ultra-cold fog made her gasp and suck in the first breath.

Her body relaxed. She sucked in another breath and he pulled a loaded injector out of an innocent-looking teak box on his console.

"I'm going to give you an injection now. It's the primary tranquilizer. Please roll up your right sleeve."

She pulled up her sleeve without opening her eyes. He aimed the injector at her arm and shot a fine spray through the pores of her skin.

He waited fifteen seconds by the clock. Her hands slid into her lap. Her breathing relaxed.

"You're doing fine. Raise your right hand and hold up two fingers."

She raised her hand and held up the first two fingers. The first drug he had given her was a mild hypnotic as well as a tranquilizer. It would wear off in two or three minutes but by that time she would be sitting in the treatment room.

He pressed a button on the console. A door opened on the right side of his office. "Stand up and follow me, please, Miss Keenan."

She opened her eyes and stood up. He led her across the office and eased her into the molded chair in the middle of the treatment room.

Straps closed around her arms and shoulders. She sprawled in the chair like a teenager and he glanced at the dials on the walls and checked out her heartbeat and blood pressure and the electrical resistance across her palms.

He picked up an injector loaded with a medium

strength psychic energizer and checked the dose in the cartridge against the printout he had left in the treatment room. "I'll be in the next room, Miss Keenan. The computer will call me if anything unusual happens. I'll be monitoring you over my screens and I'll be getting a simultaneous printout as the conversation goes on. I'll know right away if anything goes wrong. Just sit there and do whatever comes naturally."

He pulled the trigger on the injector. The drug shot into her skin and he backed away and studied the dials.

A middle-aged woman appeared on the TV screen beside the chair: a computer simulation that matched the recommendation in the diagnosis. A pleasant female voice asked Julia Keenan the first question on the program.

He stepped into the main office and the door slid shut behind him. A typer on his console had already started moving along a roll of paper. The computer would respond to the client's answers with more questions and Julia Keenan's drug-stimulated brain would begin to draw conclusions and form hypotheses whether she wanted to form them or not. The tranquilizer would weaken her resistance to self-knowledge and a process that had once taken months and even years would be compressed into three hours.

He dropped into the chair and stared at the console. He had twenty-five minutes before his next appointment. He had given Julia Keenan the normal amount of time and she had used less than half of it.

The computer could feed him a dozen scientific papers he should have read two weeks ago. He could look over the latest reports on some of his long-term patients and call up the people who were supervising their therapy if he had any questions. Sixteen people were being treated with long-term therapies he had prescribed and he usually kept track of them by putting these odd minutes to good use. He had been putting a lot of time into his political adventures but he still had one of the highest productivity rates in the city. In the thirty hours he spent in his office every week, he usually processed twenty major complaints and fifteen or twenty minor emotional upsets.

A red light glowed on his console. It stayed on for fifteen seconds and then it winked out.

"Computer. Report on the phone call last received."

"Dr. Edward Saboletsky phoned. Message. Tell him I said I'd like him to call me back as soon as he can."

He switched on the TV camera in the treatment room. A screen lit up on the left hand side of his console and he studied the figure lolling in the treatment chair.

"Computer. Phone Dr. Edward Saboletsky."

A thin young man in a neatly tailored jacket bounced onto the phone screen. Nicholson had been working with Ed Saboletsky for three years now and he had soon decided Ed would look cool and relaxed if you pulled him out of bed at four in the morning.

"Good morning," Saboletsky said. "How's it going?"

Nicholson shrugged noncommittally. "The medics claim I'm going to live."

"You're actually working already?"

"I just put a patient in the treatment room. I've got about ten minutes before I have to start getting ready for the next one."

"I called you up because I was just talking to Bob Dazella. He sounds like he's pretty worried about the possibility they may have tampered with your little psyche."

Nicholson's eye slid toward the woman sprawling in the treatment room. He squinted at the phone screen and spread his hands.

"He probably guessed I wasn't telling him the whole story. I'm afraid I've got a pretty serious problem, Ed."

"There's more to it than you've told us?"

"They hit me with a hypnotic right at the start. When I was getting inside the police car. They kept me there all night so it wouldn't show up in the tests."

"They worked you over like that just so they'd have a cover for a hypnotic?"

"They wanted to make sure I couldn't convince a jury they'd done anything else. They questioned me for three hours under the hypnotic before they started working me over. They got all the information they

77

need to type Sue. They said they'd take it out on her if I did any more work in Boyd's district."

Saboletsky winced. He stared at Nicholson as if he had just been told somebody had died and Nicholson locked his eye on the screen and squinted back at him.

"They've got her right where they want her," Nicholson said. "I've been thinking about it ever since I left that Goddamned police station and there isn't a damned thing we can do that'll give her enough protection. I can't go ahead with the project and keep her out of trouble, too."

"You're thinking about giving up the project?"

"I can't keep it up and keep her reasonably safe, too. I thought she'd be safe if we kept her over on this side of the river. But they can get her anywhere now, if they want to."

Saboletsky shook his head. They had worked with some pretty unhappy people during the last three years but this was the first time Nicholson had seen him look seriously disturbed. He was a very competent young man, but he claimed he thought of his profession as a business, and he insisted he wasn't interested in helping anybody who couldn't pay him. Nicholson had never seen his personality classification, but he was pretty certain Saboletsky was probably a G-4 or a G-5, personality classifications that were characterized by a desire for orderly serene, pleasant relationships with the world. Saboletsky worked with human beings as if he were a technician working with electronic equipment, and he had the same kind of personality many technicians seemed to have; he was reasonably contented with himself, he stayed well inside the limits of his abilities, and he usually gave people the impression he was a relaxed, easygoing man who did his work competently, made a good living and didn't knock himself out trying to dominate the universe.

"That's a big decision, Ralph."

"It's one of the worst decisions I've made in my life. I've been going round and round with it since it happened and there isn't one damned thing I can do."

"You don't think you can set up the same kind of safeguards we set up for you?"

"We set up our safeguards on the assumption they'd try to tamper with my personality. They'll get her with the same kind of trap they used on me if they go after her now, and they won't try to hit her with something we can fix up in a therapist's office. They can kill her with what they've got, Ed. And there won't be a damn bit of evidence it was murder."

"And you don't think you can set up a system that will keep her safe until after the election? How long will you have to protect her if you actually manage to win the election and boot the old cancer out of office?"

"They won't count the votes in the general election for another thirteen months."

"It still might be better than quitting. That's a big step for somebody like you, Ralph. I don't care whether you quit or not, but you shouldn't do it too hastily."

"I can't make Sue take that kind of risk. I've looked at it from every angle I can think of and there isn't one damn thing we can do that'll keep them away from her for thirteen months. Giving those bastards thirteen months is like giving them forever, with all the resources they've got."

"It's still going to have an effect on you. It's an acceptable reason for quitting, but that doesn't mean it won't throw you into a tailspin. Why don't you get together with some of the people you're working with and make absolutely sure you can't protect her before you make any final decisions? It'll only take a couple of days and it'll probably have a big effect on your feelings."

Nicholson squinted at the phone screen. His brain flipped through the people he was working with as if they were cards in a file box. Nobody who was really important would give him any problems if he told them he wanted to back out because his wife was in danger. Dazella was the only real problem. And Bob wouldn't go to a meeting that would reveal he was associated with the others.

"I'll set up a meeting right away," Nicholson said.

79

"It's going to be one of the hardest things I've ever done, but you're probably right."

"Would it make it any easier if I told Bob for you?"

"Maybe you'd better."

"I'll tell him not to bother you about it until he hears from you or me again. You're under enough stress already."

"He's going to be pretty disappointed. This business means a lot more to him than he pretends it does."

"He'd probably rather have you give up than have anything happen to Sue. I think you'd better stop by in the next day or two and let me give you a check out, too."

Nicholson's heart jumped. A haze shimmered between him and the screen.

"A check out? What for?"

"For Bob, mainly. He'll be after me from now until doomsday if I let you back out of this without looking you over first."

"You want me to fit that and a meeting into my schedule, too? What the hell do you think I do around here all day?"

"I wouldn't be doing my job if I didn't insist on it. I know your productivity record is a thing of beauty and a joy to everybody who hears about it, but I still think a check out's absolutely necessary. There's no telling what the cancers did to you while you were under the hypnotic."

Nicholson shook his head. He started to argue and then he slumped back in his chair and spread his hands. "I'll have my computer set up an appointment for a check out, too. It'll probably have to do some fancy juggling but it can probably do something."

Saboletsky glanced at his watch. "I'll see you as soon as our machines tell us we can get together, then. I've got a patient coming in now myself."

"Take it easy."

"Cheers."

The phone screen blanked. Nicholson sprawled in his chair and stared at Julia Keenan.

"Computer. Prediction program. Gruber type G-6. Nicholson, Ralph. Predict—"

He rasped out a long chain of numbers and code words. Another typer started humming on the console and he waited while the printout crept through it.

The typer stopped humming and he picked up the printout and looked it over. All the predictions for situations that looked realistic indicated Saboletsky would find out he was hiding something before he finished a check out that lasted more than twenty minutes. An injection with any of the standard drugs would bring the whole story out in the open almost immediately. The standard analytic programs would zero in on the truth as soon as he began talking about the incident.

He hunched over his desk and ran his finger down the printout. He knew the techniques Saboletsky would use and he could work out maneuvers that would help him thwart them. He would have to check out his strategy by testing it with the model of his personality stored in his computer, but Saboletsky wouldn't be dealing with a naïve patient. He knew what the therapist was going to do. If he sat down with the computer and planned every reaction in advance, there was a good chance he could—

His fist crashed against the top of the console. He raised the printout above his head with both hands and heaved it across the room as if he were heaving a rock. It fluttered frustratingly to the floor and he banged his fist against the top of the console again.

A light blinked on the console. "Mr. Ronald Shapiro is here for his appointment."

He shoved his hand across the console and switched off the screen that was monitoring Julia Keenan. Emotional reflexes took over once again. Shapiro had called him the day before and refused to tell the computer what his problem was. He had kept his screen blank and he had sounded tense and conspiratorial. He had insisted no other therapist in the city could help him.

No therapist ever put off a patient who acted like that. Most of them were just being melodramatic, but you could never be certain. A significant number were about to commit crimes of violence.

"Send Mr. Shapiro in."

The door slid open. A chunky, smooth-faced young

81

rock ambled across the room with his hands in his pockets.

The therapist stood up. "Good morning," the therapist said. "Come right in, Mr. Shaprio. Have a seat."

Shapiro stopped in front of the console. His eyes slid around the room.

"I'm afraid I'm not a patient. I talked that way on the phone because they told me that was the only way I could be sure I got in here today. A man named John Hill sent me here to give you an envelope. He said he wants you to call him."

Nicholson's face darkened. Shapiro stepped back and held up his hand.

"I don't know anything about it," Shapiro said. "All I know about this is the stuff I saw on TV. I don't even know what's in the envelope."

Nicholson held out his hand. "Where is it?"

"He said to tell you to call him first."

"Computer. Call Dr. John Hill in Washington, D.C. Dr. Hill is listed under Boyd, Congressman, Chief Psychologist."

Shapiro folded his arms over his chest. His chunky body looked muscular and well coordinated and he carried himself like a perfect example of the relaxed, well-balanced young men who spent the long afternoons of the "new leisure" working out in gymnasiums and studying the unarmed arts in dojos.

John Hill jumped onto the screen. "Good morning, Dr. Nicholson. How are you?"

"What do you want?" Nicholson said.

"I just wanted to make sure you were all right. I thought it would be a good idea if I talked to you about Ronnie's package, too. Will you hand him the envelope, please, Ronnie?"

Shapiro pulled a plastic envelope out of his pocket. Nicholson held out his hand and Shapiro gave him the envelope and stepped back another step.

He knew what it was as soon as he saw the thin sheet of green plastic inside. Drop the sheet into any home viewer and it would immediately begin screening the scene Hill had recorded.

He threw the envelope on the console. "You son of a bitch. You smelly little cancer."

"I assumed you could think of one or two things we could do to Mrs. Nicholson without any special help from me. I wanted to make especially sure you thought of that one, however. I think I forgot to mention I was recording our conversation when we were talking things over the other night."

Nicholson pulled himself erect. His face was as emotionless as a blank television screen. Anything he said would give Hill the pleasure he was looking for.

"Do you have any other messages?"

Hill smiled. "Not right now, thank you. Have a nice day now."

The screen blanked. Nicholson picked up the envelope and threw it in the incinerator beside the console.

"You can go now, Mr. Shapiro. You've run your little errand."

"You may see me around," Shapiro said. "Don't worry about it. They asked me to help you if anybody jumps you."

Nicholson froze. Hill's smiling face hung in front of his eyes.

"They told you to bodyguard for me?"

"He said you might need protection."

"And they told you to tell me they were doing it?"

"He said I'd better make sure you didn't get the wrong idea. We'd both feel pretty stupid if you noticed I was hanging around and had the cops pick me up just before you needed me."

A voice screamed in Nicholson's skull. Every cowardice made him hate himself a little more.

"What's it all about?" Shapiro said. "Who do they think's trying to get you?"

"Do what you want to," Nicholson said. "I don't know any more about it than you do."

83

VIII

The telescopic sight framed John Hill's face. His finger squeezed the trigger with the controlled, steady pressure they had taught him to use when he had tried out for the rifle team in high school. The shock of the recoil drove the back of his thumb into the anchor point under his right eye.

He took a scrambler out of a side drawer and clipped it inside the inside pocket of his jacket. The hands on the clock on his console were pointing at three P.M. Julia Keenan had gone home twenty minutes ago with one of the hospital social workers escorting her. Three other patients had come in for initial interviews. Six people had talked to his computer and been given appointments for the next day.

"Computer. Nicholson is leaving for the day. Repeat lock up program when the door closes next time."

He slumped back in his chair and watched the hands of the clock slide around the dial. The trip home stretched ahead of him as if it was going to drain him of every erg of energy stored in his muscles.

He eased himself out of the chair. His legs carried him across the office as if somebody else was moving them.

Shapiro was sitting in the waiting room with a pocket TV in his hand and an earphone plugged into his ear. Nicholson walked past him with a nod and Shapiro stood up and followed him down the hall to the elevator.

Shapiro rode the elevator with him, Shapiro followed him up the sidewalk to the corner, Shapiro got in the automated taxi behind the automated taxi that stopped for him, Shapiro followed him into his apartment building and watched him enter his apartment. . . .

His eight year old, Margaret, was playing tennis on the roof of their apartment building. He told Sue he felt like sucking in some fresh air and they stretched out on a pair of deck chairs at the edge of the tennis court and spent the afternoon cheering Margaret on and watching the younger girls scream around the rooftop tot lot. It was a bright, crisp day and the heater built into his clothes felt as snug and warm as a hot bath. A serving cart brought them snacks and a pair of happy drinks and he spread his drink over an hour and a half and turned down a second when Sue ordered another one. He had ordered the same mild happy drink he had drunk at Mead's but he was going to have to be extra cautious for a long time to come.

He glanced at his watch a little after five. "I think I'd better take a little nap before dinner, love. Do you think all you helpless womenfolk can get along without me for awhile?"

"I guess we can always call you on one of your mysterious, masculine electronic devices if something comes up we can't handle by giggling and batting our eyelashes. What do you want me to do if you're still lying there snoring like a pig when the machine finishes dinner?"

Nicholson hesitated. "I guess you'd better wake me up. I told one of the interns at the hospital I'd have a conference with him tonight."

"Tonight?"

"He called me up first thing this morning. He sounds like he's got a bad case of 'I'm in the wrong trade and I'd better get out before it's too late.' "

"And only the best known clinical psychologist in the city can possibly help him out."

"Of course."

She shook her head disgustedly. "How long do you think it'll take this time?"

He hesitated again. It had been three days since the last time they had made love and she had obviously been hoping he would be in good shape tonight. Her menstrual period was supposed to start sometime in the next day or two and she didn't like the drugs that could be used to delay it.

"It may take awhile. He sounds like he's really hanging on the edge of the cliff. I'll try to be back by midnight but I can't guarantee it."

She shook her head again. "It's too damn bad these silly kids can't work out their little problems on their own."

"I tried to get him to wait until tomorrow but he sounded like he might break down right on the phone if I didn't see him as soon as possible. Personally, I'd just as soon have us get some sleep tonight and enjoy ourselves in the morning. I don't have any appointments scheduled until ten-thirty and the other stuff I was going to do is all stuff that can wait a couple of days."

Sue looked down at her right hand and stretched. Their oldest children could get up and go about their business without them, and the baby-sitting program could take care of Ellen for a couple of hours without doing her any harm.

"That might be nice, too," Sue said.

He turned over in his chair and looked at her across the space that separated their chairs. She had put on a little extra weight as she had gotten older, and the lazy tone in her voice and the extra coating of flesh on her body aroused more simple physical lust than she had aroused when she had been ten years younger. He would have taken her downstairs and buried himself in her right now if there had been any way they could slip away from the girls.

She stretched again and he stood up and squeezed her shoulder. He ran his fist along her cheek and then he straightened up before she could get a good look at his face and headed for the elevator.

He stepped into the bathroom and checked out the medicine cabinet as soon as he entered the apartment. They had the usual supply of tranquilizers, relaxers, and stimulants, but every one of them had to be administered orally. Nothing in the cabinet could be injected into his muscles or sprayed in front of his nose while he was asleep.

Dazella probably wouldn't try anything drastic before the day Saboletsky was supposed to give him his checkup. Sue would probably hesitate for a long time before she did something that could wreck the sense of trust that kept their marriage together. But he couldn't be sure.

He left the house an hour after dinner and rode downtown in a taxi. He walked around the streets for half an hour and then he dropped into a private, enclosed booth in a bar and sipped on another glass of Gallio's Mild Joy. The warm feeling spread through his body and he slumped against the back of the booth and stared at the opposite wall from the inside of a cocoon.

The warm feeling started to ebb and he took another sip and brought it back again. He had been using TP3L for three years now and he knew the rhythm. He could spread a glass like this over forty-five minutes and remain almost continuously warm and relaxed.

He stood up and left the booth with a third of the amber-colored drink glowing in the glass. Crowds flowed around him as he trudged through the theater and bar area. Young girls attracted his attention and he found himself eyeing them with the same emotions they had aroused when he had been in the first stage of puberty and there had been no guarantee he would ever hold a naked female body in his arms. Signs pulled at his emotions with messages that had been designed by some of his more commercially minded colleagues. Computer animated cartoons pulled him to the side of the walk and held his attention with performances that were genuinely entertaining but which also aroused appetites that were supposed to draw him into the theaters and pleasure houses that lined the street for fifteen blocks.

Even the girls were using clothes and makeup that had been selected by psych technicians. The brunette coming down the street might not know why her hair was two feet long and her clothes were made out of imitation red felt, but she was dressing like that because she had gone into a beauty shop and a technician had given her a battery of tests and sold her a wardrobe and a makeup kit that were guaranteed to attract men she would like. They could even tell her if she would like the men right away or if she was supposed to see them a couple of times before she decided they weren't her type.

He turned away from Market Street and wandered into the downtown residential area—a neighborhood that had settled into its final shape in the 1970's and stayed the same ever since. High-rise apartment buildings had taken over the rest of the city as the population had boomed, but the city planners had managed to preserve the expensive town house neighborhood that had grown up in center city in the middle of the century. People still lived in three-story brick row houses in this neighborhood, and it still looked like Paris and London had probably looked in the eighteenth century. The houses were filled with gadgets but Napoleon could have walked through the quieter streets at night and convinced himself the world had hardly changed. The taxis were automated and the streets were lit by electricity instead of gas, but the houses were still made out of brick and the streets were still narrow.

Music pulled him toward a street festival on one of the side streets. The street had been blocked off and people were drinking happy drinks out of steins and dancing group dances in the middle of the street. Five archers lined up at the end of the dancing area as he walked toward it and he raised his head and watched five arrows rise toward the stars with their colored lights flashing and firework noises screaming out of their miniaturized loudspeakers.

Five more arrows shot straight up. Bursts of flashing light imitated bombs. Wings snapped out of the arrows in the dark and they swooped and turned above the street with their lights making patterns in the sky and music thundering out of their loudspeakers. The people in the street threw back their heads as they danced and the people sitting at the outdoor tables raised their steins and sang a big, happy song at the lights and music soaring above them.

He stopped twenty feet from the barrier and watched the festival from the darkness under a tree. He had always loved parties and carnivals and he thoroughly approved of the advances in party making that had taken place during the last twenty-five years. An entire party could now be staged like a big musical comedy in which every guest had a role. Guests could be mailed learning programs which could teach them their role in the party, and the learning techniques were so efficient they could even accommodate people who wandered into a street festival without any advance notice. Every street festival had a learning booth in which a guest could learn any of the songs or dances he didn't know yet—and do it with a learning program which had been designed so the learning process would be almost as much fun as the party itself.

He stood under the tree and stared at the dancing, singing people as if he were a ghost watching a scene out of his past. They had put a wall between him and everything he had ever loved. Every emotion he had ever felt had been numbed by the knowledge he had failed.

His fists clenched inside his pockets. How could any sane human being let his vanity do that to him? How could he give up everything that had been important to him merely because he was afraid somebody would discover he had failed to live up to an ideal that would have looked ridiculous to most of the people he knew?

His vanity had always been that strong, however. And he had always known it. Every time he had entered the Fifth Congressional District he had been risking all the pleasure and happiness the world could offer and running after the role he wanted to play. They had merely taken his emotions and channeled them in a new direction.

Voices rose behind him. He turned around and saw a crowd of young people standing on the corner at the end of the block. They were standing under the corner street lights and he could see the chains hanging from their necks and the silver statues of the Indian goddess of death shining at the ends of the chains. Their leader was bellowing as if he was standing on a stage, and some of the people in the front ranks looked like they were gesturing at the street festival.

Shadows moved behind some of the windows along the block. A light winked off in a house on his left.

Two big, healthy looking men slipped out of the crowd around the tables and took up positions near the barrier that separated the festival from the rest of the street.

Five more arrows shot toward the sky. Two girls stepped out of the kaligang and waved the rest of the gang on. Some of the people on the edge of the dancing area turned around and eyed the commotion.

The leader of the kaligang shouted an order in a parade ground voice. The figures on the corner snapped into a column of twos and marched across the intersection with their boots crashing on the pavement. They disappeared around the corner and the two bodyguards relaxed and turned back to the festival.

Nicholson turned away from the music and trudged down the street. He stopped at the corner and stared down the block at the tramping kalis. Most of the people in front of the gang were crossing the street as they approached. Little clumps of people were watching them from the other side of the street.

The kalis usually swaggered more than they acted, but people had learned it didn't pay to assume they were harmless. They had caught a lot of social commentators off guard when they had first strutted onto the American stage, but they were a textbook example of the cult of violent emotions and destructive acts which seemed to spring up whenever a society enjoyed a long period of peace and prosperity; they were posers at heart, but they had to back up their pose by actually doing something violent now and then.

A cold wind blew across the intersection. He turned up the heater in his jacket and settled into the warmth as if he was settling into a blanket. Every nerve in his body wanted his wife. They had been moving toward one of those moments that had made their sexual relationship a memorable experience for both of them and he was holding them back because he was afraid of his own wife.

None of the girls on the street could make him want them more than he wanted his own wife. No psych technician on the planet could give him a woman who could give him more pleasure than the woman he had lived with for twelve years. They had worked with two of the best sex counselors in the city when they had first gotten married, and they had taken advantage of most of the techniques a modern couple could use when they had all the years of a good marriage at their disposal. She knew his needs and he knew hers, and they could enjoy each other with the complete freedom of people who had cultivated their relationship with the help of psycho-active drugs and carefully programmed interpersonal exercises. Nobody watched him and kept score when he made love to Sue. They could even make love when they were angry at each other, thrusting and heaving as if each motion of their joined bodies was a blow.

He turned a corner and found himself walking past a sporting good store which had infiltrated the clothing stores and fad shops in the residential district. A girl came toward him down the street and he turned toward the window and pretended he was staring at the golf clubs and ski equipment on the left side of the display.

Bells jingled behind him. Perfume that smelled like clean, naked female flesh drifted toward him across the sidewalk. His eyes slid towwrd the girl as she walked past him.

He turned back to the window and studied the hunting weapons on the right. The owner had hung a big kali medal over the guns and the racks were arranged in front of an animated film of a kali girl and a kali rock who were shooting guns and crossbows. An arrow sliced into the flesh of a blurry animal and a mist of blood spread across the big screen.

A middle-aged couple came around the corner without warning. He turned back to the ski equipment as if he had been doing something illegal.

IX

THE PHONE LIGHT blinked five minutes after he sat down behind his console.

"Dr. Robert Dazella is calling from Washington, D.C."

His hand froze over the printout he had been picking up when the light had blinked on. He raised his head and stared at the faceless loudspeaker on the console.

"Dr. Robert Dazella is calling from Washington, D.C."

"Tell Dr. Robert Dazella I am tied up with a conference right now. Tell him I have a patient coming in five minutes from now."

The light blinked off. "Dr. Robert Dazella left a message. Please call back as soon as you can. Mr. Harold Fernandez is here for his appointment."

They could have put the call through just to see if he'd call back. They could be waiting for him with a phone call full of ambushes if he did call back. A phone conversation with Bob Dazella could be just as treacherous as a full-scale psychological check out. They could throw anything at him without warning. He wouldn't have time to think things through and spot the traps before he reacted to them. Saboletsky could go over the recording second by second and examine every little movement at his leisure.

Saboletsky had promised him Bob wouldn't call. He wouldn't have let Bob call if he didn't have a reason.

"Mr. Harold Fernandez is here for his appointment."

He took his hands away from his face. John Hill's smiling face hung in front of his eyes.

"Send Mr. Fernandez in."

The door slid open. The therapist stood up behind his console. The therapist's mouth smiled at Harold Fernandez.

"Mrs. John Buchman is here for her appointment."

"Dr. Edgar Lipman is here for his appointment."

He was a technician, not a friend. They paid him for his intelligence and his knowledge, not his kind heart or his friendly, humane personality. He wasn't there to let them know somebody cared about their problem; he was there to supervise the machines and the technicians, to answer the questions no machine could answer and ask the questions no machine could think of. He could sit there with his clinical mask frozen on his face and take them through their initial interviews at the rate of one every forty-five minutes and it wouldn't have mattered if he had been dying of cancer and burning with pain every moment. A man who couldn't talk at parties, a woman who was frightened because she kept thinking about murdering her children, a child who was failing at school even though he had a corrected IQ of one hundred and forty—they were all so many appendixes, damaged lungs, head colds and allergies.

"Dr. Robert Dazella is calling from Washington, D.C."

"Tell Dr. Dazella I've got a patient coming in. Tell him I'll call him later."

"Dr. Dazella left a message. Please call back as soon as you're free."

"Dr. Lulu Purvis is here for her appointment."

"Mrs. Helen Kane is here for her appointment."

"Dr. Robert Dazella is calling from Washington, D.C."

"Tell Dr. Dazella I've got a patient coming in! Tell him I said I'll call him back later!"

"Dr. Robert Dazella left a message. Tell him I'm making an urgent call. Tell him I have to talk to him right away."

Nicholson's hands clutched the arms of his chair. Conflicting impulses paralyzed his brain.

Saboletsky had promised him Bob wouldn't call. Saboletsky wouldn't have let Bob call him if he hadn't decided he wanted an impromptu test.

"Computer. . . . Prediction. . . . program. Gruber type. . . . G. . . . 6. Nicholson. . . . Ralph. Stress. . . . situation. Parameters. . . . Delta. . . . Four. . . . Seven. . . . Oh Nine., Gamma squared. . . . Three. . . . One. . . . Two. . . . Predict—"

The printout rolled out of the typer. A thin, bony hand reached across the console and tore it off the roll.

He had set up the equations for a generalized stress which could be avoided, but which the personality knew it would probably have to face sooner or later. And the computer had predicted the personality would tackle the stress right away at least sixty-three percent of the time.

The symbols on the paper drifted across his eyes as if he had never seen a mathematical symbol. His muscles tensed as if two different operators were trying to make them move in two different directions at the same time.

How did he know he had made the right judgment when he had picked the numbers that were supposed to describe the situation? How did he know he wasn't trying to set things up so Saboletsky would know there was something wrong?

"Computer. . . . Call Dr. Robert Dazella in Washington, D.C. . . . Tell Dr. Dazella I can talk to him right now."

The phone screen lit up. Dazella turned away from another screen on his console and eyed Nicholson across room.

"You must really be shoveling them in," Dazella said. "I've been trying to get you all morning."

"I've been trying to get my productivity rating back up to par. What's the matter?"

"I just got a call from Johnny Wyeth, the guy that's in charge of the subcommittee on police practices. He wants to know if there's any chance you can come down and testify in the next couple of days."

Nicholson tensed. His nails dug into his palms.

"Testify? In Washington?"

"Right."

He would sit in front of the committee and they would ask him questions about the incident. Three or four people would poke at him at random. There would be no way he could predict the questions they would ask him.

He smiled wryly. "I didn't realize it was such a cause célèbre."

"He thinks it would be a good idea."

"He really thinks he can accomplish something with a hearing about something like that?"

"He thinks it's a perfect example of the police taking the law into their own hands. And he thinks you're famous enough so it'll be easy to publicize."

"I'd better have him talk to my lawyers. I'm not even sure I'm supposed to talk about it with you."

"You'll do it if your lawyers say it's all right?"

94

Nicholson shrugged. "He really thinks he can do something with it?"

"He says he thinks it's one of the best cases he's had in a long time, for his purposes."

"And he's actually willing to collide with Boyd about it?"

"He asked me to act as his go-between. He wants to do it, but he doesn't want to make a move in public unless he's sure you're willing to do it."

"He sounds like he's got an awful lot of nerve."

"He's got the right kind of constituency for that kind of thing. He'd do it a lot more often if he wasn't afraid the cop lovers would start pouring a lot of money into his district."

"So he does it just enough to keep in good with the constituents that like that kind of thing. . . ."

"Right."

Nicholson shook his head. "It sounds like an awful lot of trouble just to make Wyeth look good to his constituents. I could lose a couple of days preparing for a thing like that."

"It would do me a lot of good, too. I can use a favor from him, too."

Nicholson threw back his head and laughed. "I should have known it was something like that."

"Don't laugh, friend. Some of the favors he can do for me can make life a hell of a lot easier for both of us next time the people line up in front of the voting booth."

"I still can't do it if my lawyers won't let me. Why don't you give them a call and see what they say?"

"You'll do it if they say you can?"

"If I can fit it into my damned schedule. Will he still be interested if I have to do it a couple of weeks from now?"

"He might. I'll check with your lawyers first and see what he says if they say it's all right."

"Leave a message with my machine when you get an answer. I'll let you know when I can do it as soon as my machine lines up a date."

"Have fun."

The screen blanked. Nicholson slumped back in his

chair and sank into the seat as if somebody had just cut all the wires that held him together.

"Computer. Call Harrison, Shapiro, Jenkins, and Wayne. Priority call. Advise receiver immediate answer requested."

"Dr. Danielson is ready to begin the budget committee meeting."

"Tell Dr. Danielson I'll be ready in two or three minutes. Make phone call to Harrison, Shapiro, Jenkins, and Wayne described in last order."

The young lawyer who had met him at the hospital appeared on the screen. "Good afternoon, Dr. Nicholson. What can we do for you?"

"I've got a question about my case. Are there any circumstances in which you might let me testify in public?"

The lawyer frowned. "You'd better give me the details. My first reaction is to say no, but I'd better find out what you have in mind first."

"A congressional hearing. About police practices. I can't go into detail, but a friend of mine just called me up and asked me if I could do it."

"We'd probably have to let you do it if they subpoenaed you. We wouldn't like it, but we probably wouldn't have much choice."

"But you don't think I should do it if it's a voluntary appearance? Under any circumstances?"

"Right."

Nicholson hesitated. "You should be getting a call from Congressman Dazella. I didn't think you'd tell him I could do it, but I'd appreciate it if you said no even if he gives you some good arguments in favor of it."

The lawyer's face darkened. "I'm certain we'll tell him no anyway, Dr. Nicholson. I can't imagine any circumstances in which we'd tell him we thought you should testify about your case in public."

"I'd still appreciate it if you'd tell him no even if he comes up with a plausible exception. He can be pretty persuasive. And I've got enough problems on my hands right now without trying to fit that into my schedule, too."

The lawyer smiled. "I'll see that he gets a negative answer. We may have to charge you extra for diplomatic services, but I don't really think it'll be necessary."

"Thanks a lot," Nicholson said. "I appreciate it."

The lawyer's face darkened again. "Think nothing of it, doctor. We're always glad to be of service."

The screen blanked. Nicholson slumped back in his chair again and stared at the bust of Freud on the shelf by the door.

He couldn't check his responses with the computer until he finished the budget committee meeting and got rid of the last patient on the day's list. It had been a treacherous, dangerous situation and it would be another hour before he would know if he had made the right move.

He covered his face with his hands. A hundred fingers pointed at his head.

"Computer. Call Dr. Hiram Danielson. Flash ready signal."

Four screens lit up on the console. The therapist jerked his hand at his colleagues on the hospital budget committee and Dr. Danielson began the meeting without any preliminaries. The therapist listened politely when his colleagues made their presentations and made his own presentation when the chairman called his name. The therapist frowned thoughtfully as the committee balanced an interesting research project against a piece of equipment that might add ten percent to the productivity of the technicians in the programmed environment department. Talk flowed through the winding, complicated circuits of the hospital complex as the therapist and his colleagues struggled with the eternal problem of the budget that was smaller than the need. Dr. Danielson and the therapist worked together, as they usually did, and brought their colleagues back to the immediate problem each time they started wandering into the rhetorical flights and elaborate arguments that seemed to plague every group of intellectuals when they started dealing with practical problems.

"Mr. Walter Cunningham is here for his appointment."

The therapist shook the problems of the budget out of his head. "Send him in."

A young rock stepped across the threshold. He blocked the door with his arm as it started to close and a slender, long-haired blonde slipped past him.

Nicholson jumped up. The girl was three months past seventeen and she had been studying unarmed combat in the best dojos in Philadelphia and Washington since she had been five years old. Her name was Peggy Dazella.

They fanned out and ran toward him like a pair of hunting dogs. A strange, enormous voice bellowed at them.

"Stop! Listen to me! I know what you're trying to do! I've got another patient coming in after you! She'll be messed up for life if I don't keep the appointment!"

The rock stopped on his toes with his arms spread. He glanced at Peggy Dazella and she screamed at him to keep moving and flowed toward the console without breaking her stride.

Nicholson lunged at a gas nozzle and twisted it toward her. A cloud of gas surrounded the girl's face as she came around the console with her mouth open. He jumped back and she pivoted away from the cloud and doubled over. Her knees sagged underneath her. She stumbled across the rug and collapsed on the floor with her arms folded under her head.

He lunged at the gas nozzle and pointed it at the rock. The strange voice babbled like an overstimulated manic.

"I'm not lying to you! I've got a woman coming in who's violently afraid of sex! She's coming up here for a three-hour therapy session and she'll probably never come back if she gets here and I cancel it. It took all the courage she's got to come here in the first place."

The rock lowered his hands. He stared at the unconscious girl lying on the floor and then he turned back to Nicholson. His smooth, square face looked incredibly young.

"You were making a big mistake," Nicholson said. "The people that sent you here made a big mistake. You would have done a lot of harm if I hadn't stopped her."

The rock stepped up to the girl and dropped to one knee. He reached out and touched her shoulder as if he was afraid she would have a heart attack if he moved her.

"It's only a sedative," Nicholson said. "She's just sleeping."

The rock raised his head. "We were trying to help you. They think somebody's psyched you."

"I know what they think. I've worked with her father for five years now."

"They're afraid you won't come in for a psych checkup. They've been watching you and they claim you aren't acting normal."

"I told them I'd come in as soon as I had the time. I talked to them about it yesterday and they're getting upset about it already."

"You told them you're willing to come in? You really are willing to come in?"

"I told them I'd come in as soon as I could!"

The rock shook his head. His eyes studied Nicholson's face as if he thought you could stare through a man's skull and examine his brain cells for evidence he'd been psyched.

"You'd better take her outside," Nicholson said. "She can pull herself together in the waiting room."

"I wouldn't have told them I'd do it if I'd known you had another patient coming in. They told me you didn't take patients after three o'clock."

"I'm working overtime today so I can make up for all the time I've lost. Will you please take her out of here and let me get myself pulled together before the next patient comes in? You've let them lead you into one of the stupidest tricks you'll ever get involved in."

The rock turned his head and stared at the girl stretched out beside him. A warning flickered across his face. Nicholson twisted the nozzle and a stream of gas shot out.

The rock threw himself to one side and gulped in

air through his mouth. Nicholson jerked the stick out of his belt and dropped into an on guard position.

"*Computer. Tell Mr. Shapiro—*"

A light, shadowy body landed in front of him. A kick sent pain shooting up his left leg. He lunged at an exposed stomach and the stomach slipped to one side.

A hand bounced off his wrist and shoulder. Numbness spread through his right arm. He jumped back and the screaming rock moved in again.

A flat, hard hand shot toward his stomach. Three fingers rammed into his solar plexus. The floor flew at his face as he doubled over. A club landed on the side of his neck.

X

THE CHAIR HE was sprawling in was a treatment chair. The room around him was one of his own treatment rooms. Peggy Dazella was standing in front of him and he was looking at her through a headache that felt like somebody had been banging his head against a wall.

Metal bit into his wrists when he moved his hands. He looked down his body and discovered his ankles had been handcuffed, too.

He threw his shoulders toward the left and tried to roll out of the chair. The restraints pressed against his arms and legs and he threw himself the other way and tried again.

Peggy backed away from the chair. The rock leaned on his shoulders from behind and pressed them against the back of the chair. Peggy took an injector out of the rack near the door and he slumped down in the chair and drove his shoulders against the hands bearing down on them.

Peggy turned away from him and held the injector in front of the television camera mounted over the door. Ed Saboletsky's voice rumbled out of a loudspeaker.

"It looks fine, Peggy. Let me talk to him a minute first."

Peggy turned around and waited by the rack. The rock's hands pressed into Nicholson's shoulders.

"I'm right here, Ralph," Saboletsky said. "You can't see me, unfortunately, but we patched the phone system into your console and I'm supervising the whole thing. You don't have to worry about anybody doing a damned butcher job. They were going to bring in one of their own people and do it all by themselves if I didn't help."

Nicholson eyed Peggy warily. The injector was loaded and cocked and she was only two steps away.

"She's going to give you the standard major tranquilizer," Saboletsky said. "I'm going to lead you through the same kind of program I would have used in my office. I don't like doing it this way any more than you would, Ralph, but I couldn't get them to listen to me. They think there's a good chance you've been given a posthypnotic conditioning with some kind of built-in mechanism that makes you defend it. Dazella won't let you alone until he's sure you're all right."

"I told you I'd come in as soon as we could set up a date! Couldn't you even wait three days?"

"They're afraid you might outwit the program if we gave you time to study the situation. I told them I could take that into account, but they know there's a definite possibility you could do it if we let you work it out with your model of yourself."

"You're violating every ethical rule in the book! You aren't going to learn one damned thing you wouldn't have learned if you'd waited, and you're dragging these kids into something you're going to regret for the rest of your lives once you come to your senses."

"Bob wouldn't have let you alone if we'd waited. He won't let you alone until he's sure you're all right."

"Then why the hell didn't you tell me what you were worried about? Did it ever occur to you I might have come in ahead of time without being trussed up like a Goddamned pig?"

"We were afraid to give you the warning, Ralph.

There's too many indications Bob's right. I wouldn't be doing this if I wasn't afraid he may be right."

"I told you what they did to me! You wouldn't look very normal on the printouts if you'd been through something like that either. I thought you were a competent professional, Ed. I asked you to help me with something and you're barging in here like a Goddamned kid."

"I'm doing the job you asked me to do, Ralph. This isn't a normal situation ethically. You hired me to help you with this and I'm doing the best job I can."

"I didn't hire you to come in here and strap me down like an animal. I didn't hire you to tie me up in a treatment room and work on me with a couple of untrained assistants."

"I gave Peggy a thorough briefing on the minimal help she's supposed to give me. I'll be watching the whole operation every step of the way. You're as safe as you would have been in my own office."

"Without a single trained person in hailing distance if something goes wrong? You're getting these kids into serious trouble and they don't even know it. Do you know what to do if the program accidentally touches on a sensitive area and I start going into a prepsychotic state, Peggy? It doesn't happen more than once in five thousand cases any more, but it can happen. Are you really ready to take responsibility for something like that?"

"I worked on her briefing with her all last night and most of this morning," Saboletsky said. "She knows how to handle most of the things that can go wrong. She knows how to put you out long enough to get some help from the offices near you if something comes up that she can't handle. You hired me to do a job, Ralph, and I'm doing it to the best of my ability. It may cost me the friendship of one of the best colleagues I've ever worked with, but you hired me to do it and I'm going to do it. You're as safe as you would have been in my own office. You've got nothing to fear."

"You'll be an accomplice in a criminal act if you go

ahead with this, Peggy. You'll be just as responsible for this as he is if anything goes wrong."

"She knows what she's doing, Ralph. You don't have anything to worry about and neither does she. Please go ahead and administer the injection, Peggy."

Nicholson closed his eyes. A scream twisted his face. *"Computer! Tell Mr. Shapiro to come in! Release restraints in treatment rooms two and three!"*

Peggy stepped toward the chair with the tranquilizer. The rock rested his stomach on the back of the chair and pressed down on Nicholson's shoulders with all his weight. The restraints snapped open and Nicholson lashed out with his feet and kicked Peggy in the hip.

"Shapiro! Here! In the treatment room!"

Peggy stumbled against a counter. She turned toward him with the injector clutched in her hand and he kicked at her again.

The door flew open. Shapiro leaped into the treatment room with a shriek and landed in front of the chair with his body poised for combat.

The rock's hands jumped off Nicholson's shoulders. Peggy shoved the injector into a rack and dropped into an on guard position. Shapiro hopped forward and launched a high, shrieking kick at her stomach.

Peggy jumped back. Shapiro stamped forward and she threw a kick at his kneecap and launched a screaming counterattack as he danced back.

Nicholson threw himself out of the chair and stumbled through the door. Voices shrieked and grunted behind him. Furniture scraped on the floor. He stumbled to his knees two steps from the door and Peggy broke out of the havoc in the treatment room and leaped after him.

Nicholson shuffled back to his feet and raised his hands. Peggy stopped in front of him and he stumbled back and raised his handcuffed hands above his right shoulder.

Somebody shrieked in the treatment room. Shapiro danced out of the room backward and crouched by the wall. Peggy's rock edged out of the room with his hands raised and the two young men froze in front of each other.

Peggy's eyes darted between Nicholson and the two young men eyeing each other on her left. Nicholson glanced over his shoulder and saw Saboletsky staring at them out of the big screen.

Trained muscles exploded in a spasm of violence beside the treatment room. The rock crashed into the wall head first. Shapiro pivoted toward Peggy with his hands poised.

Peggy danced across the room backward and took up a position in front of the door. Nicholson hopped toward his console and stumbled to his knees beside the chair. He yanked open the drawer that held his scrambler and came up with the weapon pointed at Peggy's face.

Saboletsky's eyes widened. "He's got a scrambler, Peggy! Look out!"

Peggy swung toward the shelf by the door and grabbed Nicholson's bust of Freud. She turned toward Nicholson with her head lowered and hurled the bust at his head with both hands.

Nicholson threw up his arms and ducked behind the console. The bust crashed into the floor behind him and he scrambled to his feet and saw Peggy bearing down on him with long, flowing strides that looked like they were taking her across a third of the room every time her feet touched the floor.

Shapiro danced toward her from the side. She pivoted toward him without breaking her stride and he jumped back as she came at him and dropped into an on guard position.

One hundred and twenty pounds of girl whirled away from Shapiro and danced toward Nicholson. He raised the scrambler and tried to aim it at the bobbing face coming toward him. Peggy's foot shot out and the scrambler flew out of his hand and bounced off the ceiling.

Shapiro stamped toward them with his hand raised. "Get out the Goddamned door, Goddamnit. What the hell are you trying to do?"

Peggy whirled on Shapiro and stamped toward him

104

with her hands poised. Shapiro dropped back and Nicholson pulled himself up and hopped between Peggy and the console.

Peggy's feet stamped again. A high female shriek filled the room. Nicholson jerked his head around and saw Peggy twisting the same nozzle he had used to put her out. The thin, focused stream of gas shot toward Shapiro as he stamped toward her. She twisted the nozzle again and a cloud of gas spread through the room as if she had just pulled the blanket off an Indian smoke signal.

Nicholson sucked in a deep breath and hopped toward the door. His manacled hands reached for the door button.

A shrieking female body crashed into his side. A hand punched him in the ribs as he stumbled onto his knees. He grunted and the sweet, pleasant smell of the gas filled his head.

He humped forward on his knees and drove his finger at the door button. His hand fell away from the door and he slumped toward the floor and sank into the kind of sleep he had been dreaming about since he had walked out of the courthouse after his hearing.

XI

CHRISTMAS LIGHTS FLOWED past the windows of the air cushion car. The rock at the wheel leaned forward in his seat and eyed the traffic on the canal as if he thought he was John F. Kennedy taking P.T. 109 into a lagoon full of Japanese destroyers. His hands twisted the wheel without warning and the car slipped out of the main traffic lane and raced down the edge of the canal toward the next landing.

The rock pushed in a pedal and reversed the fans. The car slowed down and he eased it up to the landing and turned off the engine. The car settled down on the big pontoons around its sides and the rock jumped out as soon as it touched the water.

105

The television camera over the gate pointed at the rock's face. A voice murmured a few words over the loudspeaker. The rock turned around with his left thumb hooked in his belt and jerked his other thumb at the car.

"It's all right, Dr. Nicholson. We're all clear."

Nicholson climbed out of the back seat. The gate swung open and he hurried up the landing and slipped into the yard with the rock covering his back.

Elaine Bruckner was sitting in the living room again and there was another ballet on the screen—a pre-Christmas ballet in which people in early nineteenth century clothes were gliding around in lunar gravity. Mead shook hands with them as they came through the door and Elaine Bruckner turned around in her chair and smiled at them from the living room.

"This is Robert Levalle," Nicholson said. "He's a friend of a very good friend of mine."

"It's a pleasure to meet you, Robert," Mead said. "That blonde thing in the living room is a friend of mine named Elaine Bruckner. Why don't you say hello and see if she'll fix you something chemical?"

The rock glanced at Nicholson. He had been taking his assignment very seriously ever since he and Nicholson had rendezvoused in downtown Philadelphia.

"We're going to have a private talk upstairs," Nicholson said. "I'll scream if he does anything indecent."

The rock shrugged. "You're the boss."

"How about you, Ralph?" Mead said. "Shall we pick up some supplies before we hike upstairs?"

"I think I'll say thank you and skip it this time."

"You're kicking the habit?"

"My doctor had me cut down temporarily."

"Then I guess I'll be polite and skip it, too. I could offer you something to nibble on, but my doctor's got me on a damned diet again, and I haven't found a low calorie food I like. I'm afraid I'll break down and start nibbling myself if I give you anything fit for human consumption."

"We'll suffer together. Lead the way."

Mead turned around and Nicholson followed his big back up the stairs. The lights came on as they entered the office and Mead bent over his console and fiddled with some controls that dimmed the lights and picked up the ballet on a medium size screen.

"That's a pretty light ballet," Mead said. "I can turn it off if it gets very distracting, but I don't think it'll interfere with our cerebrating."

"It'll give me something to talk to my wife about tomorrow. I would have been watching this one myself if I'd stayed home tonight."

"We have to do something if we aren't going to drink or eat. I bought a chef last year that's got every damned recipe I like stored it it and now I have to walk past the damn thing with my stomach grumbling every time I look at it."

The dancers in nineteenth century costume whirled down narrow London streets. Mead gestured at the furniture and they sat down and swiveled their chairs toward the screen.

"I'm sorry nobody called you while I was in the hospital," Nicholson said. "It was an awkward situation. I couldn't call you myself and none of the people I'm working with knew what to do."

"I tried to get in touch with you about four days after it happened. I tried to call you at your office and then I called your home and your wife told me you were in the hospital and she couldn't tell me what the problem was."

"They didn't know what to tell you. They didn't know how you'd reacted when I talked to you last time."

"And you couldn't tell them?"

"They didn't want to ask me. They were afraid it might upset the treatment."

"And you're still interested in this little political project of yours? They must have worked you over a lot worse than I realized if you couldn't talk to anybody all that time."

"They gave me some additional evidence they aren't nice people to have around. They worked me over pretty hard but the rough stuff was just a cover up. They really set that situation up so they could pull me in by myself and fool around with my emotions."

"They *psyched* you?"

"They tried to alter my emotions so I'd give up and stay out of their territory. My friends had to find out I'd been tampered with and then get me into the hospital for therapy."

"And you still want to keep on fighting them after something like that? You came back here a week after you got out of the hospital after something like that?"

"I finished putting together all the data we need in the last couple of days. I tried out five different strategies in the computer and the one I picked out gives us all the muscle we need to do it."

Mead slumped back in his chair and shook his head. A group of medieval peasants bounced onto the entertainment screen. Recorders and tambourines replaced the string orchestra that had been backing up the other dancers.

"I've set the whole thing up very carefully," Nicholson said. "I can't guarantee we'll win and I can't tell you it isn't going to be a little dangerous, too. But I've set it up so you should end up with a trivial loss or a little gain even if you lose the election. I can guarantee you won't look so bad you'll feel like you have to leave the county and I can almost guarantee you'll end up with a small following and a little more influence in the community than you have now."

Mead shook his head again. The light from the television screen played over his face like the flickering light of a fire.

"I'm not worried about my influence in the community," Mead said. "I'm worried about my influence over me. I've taken a lot of risks for things I believe in but this is something else."

"We'll both have all the safeguards I had before and some extra precautions I didn't take before, like keeping bodyguards and people we trust near us at all times. They threw a hell of a lot at me and the safeguards I set up still got me out of it. I couldn't keep them from tampering with my emotions, but it didn't do them any good in the long run either. They may make another try if we give them an opening, but I

108

think there's a good chance they'll concentrate on the struggle for the voters if we make personal attacks look difficult."

"They put you in the hospital for six weeks. They could put me out of action until the polls closed on primary day if they tried something like that on me."

"We'll go over every detail of the defense system with you until you're satisfied. We've gone over that part of the project as if we were planning a military operation. We've tried to plug up every rat hole we could think of."

"I'm not going to commit myself to this if I'm not satisfied with the precautions you've taken. I can tell you that right now. I may have exaggerated ideas about the value of my personality structure, but I like it the way it is."

"I can go over the defense system with you right now if you want to. I'd rather explain the first stage of the project first, but I can start with that, too. They couldn't have gotten through to me if I'd come here with my own car and my own driver the last time I came here. The bodyguard could have followed me when they left your house and we could have had a dozen lawyers on their necks before they could start working on me. We aren't dealing with magic. I can't guarantee this is perfectly safe, but I think there's a good chance they'll leave us alone when they see there's a good solid wall around us. I think there's a good chance they'll see personal attacks are a waste of time and try to beat us at the polls."

"Even when they know they only have to put one of us out of action for a few weeks? November is a long way off, Dr. Nicholson."

"We know we're in danger and we'll have a lot of trained people watching both of us, and Hill and Boyd will know we're well guarded. I can't promise you'll come out of this without a scratch, Dr. Mead. I can't guarantee the plan I've worked out will be a hundred percent success. We're dealing with some tough, shrewd customers and we've got less time than I'd hoped we would have. The program I've worked out gives us a reasonable chance, however. And it does it with a minimum risk to everybody involved. The first stage won't even look like it has anything to do with politics as far as the average voter is concerned. We'll start the campaign with a project that's primarily designed to bring you plenty of public attention. You're already well known around here, but this will get you to the point where you'll be as well known as a congressional candidate should be. It'll attract some of the supporters you'll need later on, and it'll associate you with a good issue, too. An issue you can use in the campaign if the results of the first stage indicate it would be a good idea. An issue that cuts across party lines and appeals to a lot of voters."

"It wouldn't happen to be something I can pretend I believe in, too, would it? Or is that too much to hope for nowadays?"

"It's the youthful vandalism and violence issue. We'll start the campaign by organizing an unarmed citizens group to patrol the county—with you as the chief organizer and the man in charge."

Mead's eyebrows rose. "Your model indicates we can win voters with a project like that?"

"It's a touchy issue in the campaign. It can backfire against you if you try to use it in the wrong situation. But the model indicates you'll win more voters than you'll lose, and you'll be reaching them with an issue that really means something to them, too. And we'll also have the advantage in that we'll be attacking Boyd with a social issue he hasn't handled very well. All the standard indicators indicate his police have been pretty inefficient crime fighters, probably because he's been primarily interested in picking cops he can conrol."

"We tried to bring that issue up when we started that reform organization. We put out a platform that said we should either get more cops or start a citizens' patrol, and it looked to me like we got trounced by everybody in the county that paid any attention to us. We got more phone calls and more public reactions on that issue than we got from anything else we ever said."

"From individuals or from the media?"

"From both. The group didn't attract that much attention anyway, but I think most of the people involved in it decided this was a bad place to bring something like that up."

"That's just the kind of reaction you should get if Hill's model of the county indicates you've got a good issue. The model I'm using indicates the project will be supported by a big minority, and a majority will at least tolerate it, and I suspect the figures were the same when your reform group brought it up, too. Hill could have thrown up a smoke screen just to make sure the people in the reform movement dropped the idea before they found out they had a good issue. He's got a lot of influence over the local media and he can make sure the people who'll react against something like that will hear about it right away. He can see that it's presented in a way that'll guarantee most of them will react against it. It's a bad issue if it's played wrong and it's a good issue if you hit the right people with the right approach."

"And you know exactly who we should hit and exactly how to hit them."

"The model I'm putting together isn't as detailed and precise as Hill's model. I can't accumulate the kind of data he can collect, and I've filled in some of the gaps with general sociological data, the fact that so many people in a certain age group feel a certain way, and so on. We can't pinpoint individuals the way he can, but we can design appeals that will bring in certain types of people, and we can focus the appeals on areas where those types tend to live. And all my calculations indicate we'll get a solid response. Hill will counterattack and try to stop us, but the people we need are there and we can reach them."

Mead shook his head. He stared at the screen with his head hunched between his big shoulders and Nicholson watched him out of the corner of his eye.

"I'm beginning to understand how my elders felt when Armstrong and Aldrin landed on the moon," Mead said.

"In what regard?"

"Everybody I knew who was over thirty kept talking about the contrast between the calm way the astronauts talked and the size of the thing they were doing. If we ever let ourselves react to the way we're twisting people's emotions, we'd both be screaming like we were looking at a row of corpses."

"We're going to *be* a row of corpses emotionally if somebody doesn't do something about these cancers."

"I still feel like screaming every time you start talking about the details of this thing. It may be the only way we can do something about it. But it's still the most revolting thing I've ever seriously considered doing."

Nicholson spread his hands. He was still certain Mead was politically hungry. and he was almost certain he was the kind of amateur politician Bob Dazella was always complaining about—the kind of man who had to appease his conscience by letting everybody know how much it hurt him when he did something dirty. But that kind of man had to be handled carefully.

The whole first stage of the project was really an attempt to hook Mead by giving him a taste of power and leadership. He was certain Mead would be willing to take some big risks once he had experienced some of the political success he had dreamed about all these years. But the whole project would collapse if he made a false move now and scared Mead away before he even smelled the carrot.

"It revolts me just as much as it revolts you," Nicholson said. "They're taking some of the most valuable knowledge men have ever possessed and they're using it to destroy everything that makes human society valuable. We aren't going to do one thing that will cause anybody any serious harm, however. Nothing we're going to do will have any permanent effect on any voter in this county. The only long-term effect we'll have on their lives will be the effect we'll have if we win. We'l be getting them out of the hands of a sadistic little bastard who's using them like private toys he can play with any time he feels like making somebody miserable. I've seen John Hill in action. He isn't in this just to keep himself and Boyd in Washington. He had a dozen tricks he could have used to knock me out of the game. He picked the one that would hurt me the most, and added a few little touches so he could get more fun out of it. I was probably on the verge of suicide when my friends rescued me—and he's probably playing little tricks like that on some of the people in Windham County, too."

"A real bad guy, huh? The kind that justifies anything we feel like doing."

"He destroyed my self-esteem," Nicholson said. "Hill had a dozen ways he could get at me but he 'picked the filthiest trick on the list. He put me in a situation where I'd do something that would make me hate myself more than anything I've ever done. He knew what he needed to make me do and he knew exactly how to make me do it. And he made it pretty damned clear he was enjoying every moment of it."

Mead's head jerked. He turned around in his chair and stared at Nicholson's face.

"He rubbed it in after it was over," Nicholson said. "He called me up at my office a couple of days later and got some extra laughs out of it then, too. A twelve-man therapeutic crew had to work on me every minute of that six weeks to get me to the point where I didn't feel like I was sharing my skull with a reptile —and I'm still not sure they succeeded."

"And you came back here after they did something like that?"

"I'm not going to sit over there on the other side of the river and do nothing when I know a man like that is playing games with the personalities of half a million human beings."

Trumpets blared on the loudspeaker system. The dancers on the screen broke into a frenzy of color and movement. Mead turned back to the screen and Nicholson watched the emotions slide across his face.

"We're just asking you to try the first stage of the project," Nicholson said. "You don't have to commit yourself to anything more than that. You'll get a good look at their strength and you'll see just how much we can do when we're actually working against them, and you'll still be able to back out if you decide you shouldn't keep it up. I can't tell you it isn't a dangerous thing to do. We'll make it as safe as we can, but it's still going to be dangerous. But you'll never have a better chance to do more good for more people."

Mead shook his head. He stared at the bouncing figures on the screen and Nicholson shut up and waited.

"Every time you come here I seem to hear another horror story," Mead said.

"The best argument in favor of getting rid of these cancers is their own actions. I wouldn't have come back here if Hill hadn't convinced me he's even worse than I thought he was."

"I've seen too many people get sucked into things they regretted because somebody told them a lot of atrocity stories, and they decided they were fighting absolute evil."

"John Hill has a long way to go before anyone can claim he's absolute evil. Somebody is going to be playing around with the voter's personalities whether we do anything or not. We can fight Boyd this way or we can let Hill play games with half a million people. Those are the only options we've got."

"And you can back that up with evidence a layman can understand? You can show me evidence I can examine critically?"

"I can go over all my work with you whenever you want to. Anybody with your background can understand it well enough to criticize it, with a little effort."

"Suppose I go over it with you and decide you're right. Suppose I tell you I still have serious reservations about the whole thing and that I might back out of it after the first stage even if you achieve everything you're trying to achieve and prove you can really beat the hell out of the bastards. Would you still be willing to go ahead with it on those terms?"

Nicholson frowned. "I shouldn't go into it if I don't have a candidate who's more committed to it than that. We'll look the whole thing over at the end of the first stage, but you'll be the key man in the whole operation. I shouldn't go into it with a candidate who may not stick with it if we do a good job."

"I can't do it on any other terms. I'm not going to

lead you on. You can damn me for a moralistic fool if you want to, but I wouldn't be telling you the truth if I didn't warn you I may not be able to stomach it once I really find myself helping you manipulate people."

"We'll be stuck without a candidate two months before the filing date if you back out. Hill will have another two years to dig in."

"It's the best I can do for you. I wouldn't be honest if I told you anything else."

Nicholson slumped back in his chair. He stared at the screen as if he had just been defeated and pretended he was thinking.

"I'm being as honest with you as I can be," Mead said. "I'm trying to keep this as open as I can."

"I'm going to be taking a lot of risks for this. I've seen what the cancers can do. I'd hate to put myself in a position like that and then have somebody I needed shrug it all off and leave me with nothing."

"Nobody's going to shrug it off. I wouldn't think very much of myself if I treated your sacrifices as if they were trivial."

"You'll take all the dangers I'm running into account when you make up your mind? You'll talk it over with me and let me show you my side of the question again?"

"I'll back out of it if it looks too dangerous and I'll back out of it if I decide I can't be a party to the kind of things you feel you have to do. I may back out of it because I'm scared out of my wits, too, but that's a risk you'll be running with anybody you pick."

Nicholson smiled politely. He stared at the screen a moment longer and then he shrugged resignedly.

"I guess we'll just have to work together on that basis then. I wouldn't have done it six weeks ago, but I don't really have much of a choice. I can't find another candidate and get him started between now and May."

XII

Two girls from Peggy Dazella's dojo gang were standing in front of her parents' Philadelphia house when Peggy and Harry climbed out of the car they had rented in Wilmington. Two cars came around the corner as they started up the walk and four rocks from the dojo gang threw open the doors and bounced out as if they were coming to a party.

Faint animal smells hit them as soon as they entered the house. Four cages and four boxes had been arranged on the living room floor and the animals in the cages started jumping and yapping as soon as they saw them.

A girl and a rock ran up to the cages and knelt in front of them. The animals smiled back with their tongues hanging out and the girl and the rock oohed and aahed.

"Look at those big heads," the girl said. "They must be geniuses."

"They're the best ones I've seen yet. Look at the way they're looking at us."

Two animals tapped on the bars of their cages and pointed at the locks with their forepaws. They looked like small red foxes, but their heads were about fifty percent bigger than a fox's head, and their snouts were shorter.

"They're supposed to be a little smarter than a chimp," Peggy said. "And they're supposed to have better reflexes, too."

The rock stuck his finger inside the cage and scratched an animal behind the ear. "I hope nobody hurts them."

Harry ripped back the strip on one of the plastic boxes. He pulled out a gadget that looked like a toy racing car with oversize wheels and the rest of the gang turned away from the animals.

A rock shook his head. "Some cancer damned sure

didn't worry about his expense account when he bought those, either."

A tall, red-haired girl dropped to her knees beside one of the cages. She stuck her hand inside the cage and the animal arched its back and rubbed its head against her palm.

"How come we're using the animals and the cars, too, Harry? It looks like they could both do the job by themselves."

"It's a safety factor," Harry said. "The coppies may have a quick way to stop one of them but they shouldn't be set up for both."

"I hope the cancers smash up the cars instead of the foxes."

A rock opened up another box and pulled out another miniature car. He looked it over with an expert eye and another rock crowded in beside him.

"Are you really sure anybody's going to believe this is just some young hoodlum's prank, Peg?"

"The people that hired us to do this claim nobody'll ever doubt it. It's a little extreme but people have done things just as complicated in other areas."

"It's a hell of a way to work your way through graduate school."

Peggy walked over to a control panel and flipped on the music she had programmed on Friday. Gold and brown earth colors started flowing across two walls. A door opened in a console behind the bar and a line of happy drinks marched out like soldiers marching out of a mechanical clock.

The red-haired girl strolled toward the bar and the rest of the gang fell in after her. Hands reached for drinks. The scent generator came in on cue and the smell of pine trees and snow mingled with the faint odor from the animals.

"It's a good joke anyway," one of the rocks said. "I wouldn't want anybody doing it to me, but the cancer who thought it up's a pure genius."

The red-haired girl shrugged. "We may even pick up a few pointers while we're at it. It never hurts to learn something from your elders."

The odor drifting out of the scent generators changed

into something that couldn't be associated with any particular memory. Harry glanced at Peggy and she looked back at him over her glass. The dojo gang had been her primary extra-familial social unit for three years now, but Harry was the only other person in the group who knew why they were doing this. Peggy had wanted to tell the rest of them the whole story, but Harry had convinced her it would be a bad idea, and she had left the recruiting up to him. She was a better karate player than he was, but they both knew he knew more about handling people.

Harry gave them the word a little after eight. They lined up their boxes and cages and the teams left the house ten minutes apart. Peggy checked out the lights and the doors a few minutes after eight-thirty and she and Harry stepped outside and activated the lock on the front door.

It had been a cold, gray Sunday afternoon when they had left Washington on the tube train, and now it was a cold winter night in Philadelphia. Peggy drove the rented car through the light traffic on the streets and Harry unpacked the recording equipment and started arranging it on the front seat. The mutated animal sat up in its cage in the back seat and stared out the one-way window like a family dog on an outing.

"I hope my father isn't sitting in front of the phone giving himself an ulcer," Peggy said.

"We picked ourselves a nice dark night anyway. We'll probably cruise right in and get back to Washington before they even know we're here."

"I hope so."

She turned into the approach to one of the bridges that spanned the Delaware River and they put the toll on Harry's credit card and rolled across the bridge into New Jersey. Harry checked out the printout Nicholson had given them and Peggy slipped into the maze of expressways that crossed Windham County.

"We're supposed to cruise up Morris Street from Columbia Avenue to Washington Avenue," Harry said. "It's about a five block stretch. Then we leave Hanover and hit a four block stretch in Cheshire."

"I hope they aren't all watching television."

"I just hope your friend Nicholson knows what he's doing. I'd hate to pull a dirty trick like this and go home without accomplishing anything."

Morris Street was a narrow street lined with the Mediterranean style row houses that had become popular in the 1980's. Anonymous white stucco fronts faced the narrow sidewalks, and the yards and gardens were tucked into neat, walled patios in the back. They cruised up the five blocks marked on their printout and Peggy turned off Morris Street and started circling back toward the beginning of the stretch.

Harry slipped a pair of earphones over his head and pointed a mike at the car in front of them. "I'll let you listen in if I pick up something good, love."

"You can have it all to yourself, lover. The less I hear of that garbage, the better I'll sleep tomorrow night."

She turned onto Morris Street. Two people were walking their pets on the first block. A couple of cars were cruising up the street ahead of them.

Harry pointed the mike at the first house on the block. A kid's voice said something about a TV show and he swung the mike toward the next house.

. . . just writing my mother. You wouldn't feel like playing chess, would you?

It's only about a week away. Relax.

When do we put the tree up?

The day after tomorrow. We'll go get it tomorrow night.

How big is it going to be?

A light flashed in the mirror. A car had turned onto Morris Street about six blocks behind them.

Goddamnit, Vickie. I don't care what you think. I only make twenty thousand lousy dollars a year, damnit. If your mother wants to see us for Christmas so Goddamned bad, why the hell can't she come here?

I haven't been home for Christmas in two years. We saw your parents last year, and my mother's been sitting alone home two years in a row. Your mother's still got your father. My mother doesn't have anybody in the world but me.

"Slow down."

Peggy eased up on the motor. The car behind her was about two blocks away.

Then why the hell can't she come here? She's living off the fat of the land on that Goddamned social security we're paying for and she can't even fly two thousand miles to see her own grandchildren?

Peggy studied the car closing in behind them. The headlights hid most of the details but Nicholson had assured her the police cars in Windham County all had red flashers on their roofs.

You know damned well she can't afford to pay her plane fare here and keep up her medical bills, too.

Then how come she manages to keep on buying happy drinks? If she's so Goddamned sick, why doesn't she take some of that money she spends on happy drinks and—

What do you expect her to do? Sit in that apartment all day and twiddle her thumbs?

Any woman who can afford to keep herself polluted all day can damn well afford to pay her own damned plane fare. If she was my mother, I'd—

The house Harry was listening to was fifty feet behind the car. The car that had been pulling up behind them had slowed down and started creeping down the narrow street with its front bumper a car length behind them.

Peggy pulled into the first empty parking space. The driver behind them shoved in his power pedal and shot past them. She leaned back in the seat and Harry pointed the mike at the houses on the other side of the street.

Garbled conversations reached him from the bottom floors of the first two houses. He swung the mike across the next house and his hand stopped at the second floor.

How's that?

Mmmmm.

Want me to do it again?

Uh-huh.

Peggy glanced at Harry's face and shook her head. She turned away from him and stared at the dark sidewalk on the other side of the street.

"Let's go," Harry said.

They turned away from the last neighborhood on their list at one-thirty in the morning. Peggy turned onto one of the main expressways and Harry switched on the playback and started editing the cubes in his recorder. He took off his earphones a little before two-thirty and Peggy changed course at the next cloverleaf and headed back to Hanover.

She turned onto Morris Street two blocks from the beginning of their target area. Harry picked up a miniature car and snapped a loaded speaker unit into the cargo compartment.

"Stop near the house where we made our first stop," Harry said.

The "fox" stirred in its cage. Peggy stopped the car in front of a house with a big tree in front of it and Harry pushed open the door and checked out the street.

His back tingled as he slipped out of the car. He laid the miniature car in the shadow between the tree and the house and twisted the two dials that programmed the guidance system. A glint of reflected light caught his eye as he stood up and he made himself squat in front of the robot again and push it out of the light.

Peggy hissed. He looked back and she jabbed her finger at the street behind her. A pair of headlights had turned the corner two blocks away.

He slipped inside the car and closed the door as if he had been stepping out of a sick room. They turned off Morris Street at the next corner and Peggy slowed down and watched the rear view mirror.

A car passed the corner behind them and continued up Morris Street. Peggy pushed in the power pedal and they cruised toward the next stop light.

"How did it look?" Peggy said. "Should we go back and take another look at it?"

"It looked fine to me. The less time we spend on the streets where we actually drop the damned things, the better."

She turned left at the next stop light and headed toward the expressway that would take them to Cheshire. Harry slumped down in his seat and Peggy took her hand off the wheel and patted his leg.

"Why don't I drop the next one?" Peggy said. "We can pull over before we hit the expressway and you can take the wheel."

"I'm all right. You get a little tense when you're actually out there, but it only lasts a minute."

"We may as well spread the stress around."

"We finished the worst part of this job when we stopped making the damned recordings. The next time we do something like this, remind me to let you do the recording when we're doing that part."

"I couldn't have done that part of it if somebody had offered me a couple of million dollars. I would have thrown the mike away six hours ago."

"It wasn't one damned bit easier for me either, believe me. I thought Nicholson was a hard rock to dance with when we took him on in his office. But anybody who'd think up a thing like this just to push a political candidate doesn't care what he does to get what he wants."

"We aren't doing anything Boyd's people don't do all the time. They may have a dozen cars cruising around spying on people right now."

"It still makes me feel like I need a bath."

XIII

NICHOLSON SWITCHED ON a Windham County TV station as soon as his alarm tingled his wrist. He watched the news as he ate breakfast with Sue, and then he took a taxi to his office and turned on two news programs and a scrambled conference call that put him in touch with Sue and Mead.

The loudspeakers had started broadcasting their recordings right about the time most of the people in the target neighborhoods had started getting up. The newscasts were full of policemen chasing cunning animals and high-speed robot cars. The cops had dogs and gas but most of the pictures looked like updated versions of an old silent movie comedy, with the loudspeakers booming intimate conversations over a two block radius all the time the cops were making fools of themselves.

"It looks like we're getting a pretty strong reaction," Nicholson said. "The TV people are giving it a bigger play than I thought they would."

"I notice they're letting some of the stuff on the recordings slip past their monitors," Mead said.

"Mmmm."

"How about the statement?" Sue said. "Do you think you're going to want any changes?"

"We'd better put it on the air a little later than we've been planning to. They're going to be pretty excited about this. It might look a little too pat if we came on too soon."

Mead shook his head. "You might know the media would eat something like this up."

"It's their kind of thing," Nicholson said.

"There's nothing like putting out a little rotten meat if you want to attract vultures. When do you think you want me to start calling people?"

"It looks like you can probably start in about twenty minutes. How many people do you have on your list?"

"About thirty."

"The big problem will probably be avoiding the impression you were just waiting for something like this to happen. That's the only thing I'm worried about right now. We're going to be dealing with some pretty intense reactions. We have to handle them pretty carefully."

Mead nodded and turned back to his news screens. He had already sounded out some of the people who might be interested in starting a citizens' patrol, and he was supposed to call them up and tell them this incident had finally convinced him he should go ahead.

Nicholson slumped back in his chair and gave the computer a series of instructions, his quantified, subjective impressions of the events on the screens. They had started manipulating the real situation, but the reactions they were getting were also giving him new information he could feed into his model.

Pictures and numbers slid along his screens as if he was sitting in the control room of an old-fashioned military command post. Nicholson had studied the history of political campaigns when he had first become active in politics and he had often wondered how old-fashioned politicians could have had the illusion they were in control of the polittcal situation. They had talked about political "strategy" but their knowledge of the voters had been so limited they had been operating in almost total darkness, and they had depended on the cooperation of thousands of restless, self-centered political workers, who had been almost as hard to control as the voters. Even today, in his campaigns with Dazella, he had manipulated the situation by manipulating three hundred volunteer workers who had been constantly pulling stunts that could have knocked the whole campaign out of orbit.

This campaign was thoroughly automated and up-to-date. He and Hill were engaged in a contest that was as personal as a game of chess.

The sheriff of Windham County came on TV at noon and let the good citizens of his bailiwick know his men had the problem under control. Sheriff Zellman was a thin, scholarly looking man who had probably been picked for the job because he looked trustworthy and comfortable, but this time even the TV interviewer looked a little critical. The station was controlled by Boyd's political allies, but they couldn't let it look like they were letting the cops off easy if the public reaction looked like it might be pretty intense.

"This whole escapade was obviously planned by people who had some unusual resources," Sheriff Zellman said. "I can't emphasize that too much. We're passing all our information on to Washington and I won't be very surprised if we discover the vandals had to cross a state line to get here. I can't believe anybody who lives in this area would be foolish enough to do something like this. It would be too easy to track them down if we thought we could confine the search to people who live in the county."

Sue glanced at Nicholson across the three miles that separated their home and his office. He waved at her reassuringly and she turned back to her news screen.

"Suppose they did come from outside the county, Sheriff Zellman. Do you think there's still a good chance you'll be able to track them down?"

The sheriff stuck his hands in his pockets and frowned over his glasses, as if he was discussing his last lecture with a couple of students. "I'd say there's a very good chance we can track them down, all things considered. We've got some of their equipment in custody and we'll have all the resources of the Federal Bureau of Investigation at our disposal. Once we trace that equipment back to the manufacturer, they shouldn't stand a chance."

"It's a long, cold trail," Nicholson said. "My contact man told me it goes underground in three different places."

"I hope so," Sue said.

"Do you have any idea why they might have picked our area, sheriff?"

"It would probably take a psychologist to figure that out, Steve. And I suspect he might end up deciding it was a random choice. The world is full of people who think something like this is funny. We all know we're living in an era when many of them have the money to travel halfway across the United States to do something like this. This looks like a particularly clever piece of work, but it's only a little more expensive than some of the vandalism we've put up with in this county in the past. This kind of random, pointless violence is one of the leading social problems of our time, in my opinion. And I'm afraid we're probably going to be putting up with it as long as the courts keep on being lenient with the kind of people who do these things. I don't consider something like this a prank myself, and I don't see why the courts should consider it a prank, either. The mental anguish these people have inflicted on dozens of innocent human beings is just as real as anything they could have done with a knife or a gun."

"That's about what I thought that phony bastard

would say," Mead said. "I notice he didn't mention that he and his buddies listen in on people all the time."

"It probably slipped his mind," Sue said.

Nicholson glanced at the clock. "Computer. Conduct survey. Sample Pattern One. Question One— What do you think about police handling of the vandalism which took place this morning? Question Two— Do you think anything can be done to stop this vandalism? If so, what? End of questions. Special instructions. Have interviewee rate answer to question one on rate scale one. Replay first five answers to question two. Follow replay with replay of random sample of answers to question two. Replay one answer in seven for random sample."

Fifteen phones buzzed in selected homes in Windham County. A pretty girl appeared on each phone screen and told the householder she was calling for Public Opinion Survey Corporation on behalf of a local social research group which wanted to know the householder's opinion about the recent vandalism in Windham County. The computer filed fifteen answers in its memory, fifteen phones rang again, and fifteen simulated girls interviewed fifteen more people.

A woman's face appeared on a ten-centimeter screen on Nicholson's console. The computer-controlled lighting in her house automatically flattered her face as she turned her head, but she looked like she was probably a housewife in her late forties. The printed line on the bottom of the screen said she lived in Cheshire, on one of the blocks that had been hit by the pranksters, and that she had answered the first question by giving the police a good rating for their handling of the incident.

"We aren't going to stop these outrages until the courts stop coddling these people and parents start controlling their children again," the woman said. "I don't care what anybody says. We're raising up a generation of children without an ounce of social responsibility. They've been given everything they've ever wanted all their lives, and not one of them seems to understand they're supposed to give something back."

The woman's face faded. A round-faced man took

her place. The type on the screen advised Nicholson he was watching an interview with a man who lived a mile from the nearest vandalism, and that the man thought the police had done a good job.

"I'm no expert on this subject," the man said. "But it looks to me like we need more police. Either that or somebody should do something about the way the police are deployed. I hope the police catch these people but I'd be a lot happier if they'd prevented the whole thing in the first place."

A busty young woman with a baby in her arms replaced the man. She had told the computer she thought the police had done a good job, but she was obviously upset.

"I don't know what the solution is. I just know we'd better get somebody in office who can do something about this kind of nonsense before our whole society falls apart. We're going to find ourselves in the middle of the worst catastrophe in history if we don't start making some serious changes soon. The people who keep telling us we can live with things like this are feeding themselves the biggest delusion anybody's tried to swallow yet."

The computer interviewed two hundred people and the final tally flashed on the screen half an hour after he had ordered the survey. Ten percent of the people thought the police had done an excellent job, but the majority only gave them a fair to good rating. Most of the answers to the second question indicated people were more interested in prevention than in putting people in jail after the crime had taken place.

He tapped a key on his console and screened Mead's report on the three phone calls Mead had made while the computer had been conducting the survey. Mead turned away from the phone he was using for his other calls and Nicholson jerked his hand at him.

"How's it look?" Mead said.

"It looks like we're getting exactly the kind of response we wanted. I think we'll run your statement at one. We'll get off to a fairly early start and then we'll run it again in the evening."

"The guys I've talked to so far sound like they're

ready to hit the streets tonight. If they ever find out who did that, they'll lynch him."

"That's about how the survey looked, too. It looks like you can really let them know you're angry when you tape the statement. I don't think we should give them the impression you're so angry you've lost control of yourself, but I think you can let them know you're just as disturbed as they are."

"I'll pretend Boyd's people did the whole thing."

Sue phoned a contact in the ad business and had him buy time on the cheapest TV station in Windham County. She started putting Mead through a rehearsal of his statement and Nicholson dropped out of the conference call.

"Computer. Lecture backlog."

A professor from the University of California appeared on one of his screens and started delivering a lecture on some recent research on biological clocks and their effect on human response to social symbols. His nerves were being bombarded with stimuli but he was three weeks behind in his professional literature and he would be an idiot if he sat here chewing his fingernails. Mead sounded like he might be having second thoughts again, but there wasn't a damned thing he could do about it. He had decided they should tell Mead they had arranged the prank and now he would just have to live with the decision. All his knowledge of Mead's personality had indicated Mead would have walked out at once if he had discovered they had set up the prank without telling him about it. Mead was looking for evidence he was being manipulated. He might be revolted by the prank now that he could see the results on TV but he knew he had agreed to it in advance. They would just have to cross their fingers and hope he would stay in line.

A red light flashed on his console at twelve-thirty. He turned on the conference call and Sue held up a cube.

"I think we got a good take," Sue said.

"Let's see."

She dropped the cube in a player on her console and Mead's image took her place on the screen. His

128

skin looked slightly moist—one of Sue's favorite touches —and his face and shoulders filled the screen as if he was making a personal phone call.

Nicholson glanced at the screen that showed him Mead's current image. Mead had already seen the recording at least once but he was leaning forward in his chair and staring at the replay as if he had never seen himself before.

The sweaty face and the bull neck were a nice counterpoint to the understatement of the speech itself. Mead looked like a powerful, angry man, but his words were reasonable and Sue had avoided all the ideas that could have set off strong emotional reactions. There was no criticism of the police in the statement, and there was no mention of his personal disgust with the amorality and self-centered hedonism of today's youth. He was a reasonable, respectable citizen who had decided he should form a citizens' patrol and he hoped other reasonable, law-abiding citizens would call up and volunteer. But his face and his muscular body suggested there was a good chance he was going to offer his recruits something a little more aggressive.

Sue came back on the screen as soon as the recording ended. She glanced at Nicholson and he nodded approvingly.

"It looks fine," Nicholson said. "It looks like we can run it just as it is."

"I still don't like that damned sweat oil," Mead said. "It seems like a pretty phony trick to me."

"It looked natural enough on the screen. It's the quickest way to show people you're upset."

"It still seemed phony. I'll be damned if I'd do something like that if this was an ordinary commercial operation."

Sue phoned the announcement to her contact and they watched it again when the station broadcast it at one. The computer started selecting homes from the model as soon as the announcement went off the air, and the reactions of the people who were being phoned started flowing onto Nicholson's screens. Very few people had seen the statement when it had actually been broadcast, but the computer was supposed to repeat it during each phone call if the person who answered the phone responded to the initial hooker.

"We'll probably get a slow response at first," Nicholson said. "The pace will probably pick up as the afternoon goes on. We set up the phone program so it would take into account the fact that a lot of adults will still be out to work in a lot of homes. We could probably cut our phone bill by seventy percent if we could pinpoint the best prospects as precisely as Hill can probably pinpoint them with his model."

"Can you give me an estimate on the kind of response we can expect?" Mead said.

Nicholson hesitated. He wanted to impress Mead with his ability to make accurate predictions but he had to be careful. The results could vary by twenty percent in either direction. The witch doctor would look pretty silly if he said they were going to get two hundred and twenty volunteers and they only got a hundred and sixty.

"I'm hoping we'll get two hundred volunteers by the end of the evening. The big unknowns in the equations are Hill's counterattack and the fact that I'm still refining our model and I still don't know exactly how much it's in error. I'm assuming Hill didn't realize this was part of our campaign strategy until you went on the air. He can start preparing his counterattack right away, but we probably won't feel the real impact until this evening."

"And you're hoping we'll have two hundred volunteers after the counterattack or before?"

"After."

The numbers on his lower right hand screen started changing. Nicholson stopped to watch and Sue and Mead waited.

"We've got four volunteers so far," Nicholson said. "The model predicted we'd have three at this stage."

"What's that come to?" Mead said. "About one volunteer every fifty calls?"

"We'll probably do about ten percent better than that as the day wears on. We'll probably get a steady buildup for the rest of the day and then we'll lose some ground again when they counterattack."

130

He slouched back in his chair and tried to look relaxed. His voice had sounded cool and expert but he could feel himself tense every time the numbers changed. Peggy's dojo gang was supposed to pull off a second prank if it looked like the voters needed another push, and he was almost certain they would lose Mead if he told her to go ahead with it. Mead knew about the second prank, too, but he was certain Mead was hoping they wouldn't need it. The gang was supposed to plant gas generators which would cover three big areas with the commoner psycho-active gases.

He waved his hand casually. "The next couple of hours may get pretty dull. I'll have to keep an eye on the screens in case anything goes wrong, but we're probably going to spend the rest of the afternoon sitting in front of the screens watching the numbers change."

XIV

THE COUNTERATTACK STARTED at two-thirty. Sheriff Zellman held an informal press conference in the hall outside his office and Sue picked it up on the local news at three.

It was a typical Zellman statement. The sheriff was leaning against a door with his hands in his pockets and he kept lowering his head and looking over his glasses as he talked. Nobody who watched him could have believed this kindly, reasonable sociologist would ever let his cops help a young sadist beat a man up. He knew people were pretty upset about this thing and he had to admit he was pretty upset himself. But this was no time to form "vigilante" groups. They weren't going to stop lawlessness by trying to fight it outside the law.

"That's just like that sneaky bastard," Mead said. "Talk like you're everybody's image of the kindly old professor. And slip in a little slander as if it's an obvious

131

fact. They could replace that guy with a computer simulation and nobody'd notice the difference."

Nicholson dropped out of the conference call and went on watching lectures with one eye on the tallies. Zellman had reacted to Mead's statement in an hour and a half. By now Boyd's computer had probably printed up a list of the people who would probably be attracted to Mead's organization. Copies of the list would be transmitted to committeemen and block captains. Local party workers would call the people on the list and urge them not to join the "vigilante" group. In many cases the list would probably tell them the slant they should take, too. Many prospective volunteers would be dissuaded by the fact that somebody had merely called them up and talked to them, and Hill had the advantage that he knew which people had been tempted by Mead's announcement. Few of his workers would know why they were saying the things they were saying, of course. But few of them would care, either. Party workers could be selected by the computer, too; by now, Hill probably had hundreds of workers who would do what they were told to do, and who would report the results to headquarters in exactly the same way they reported all the bits of apparently meaningless data they had been collecting since Hill had started running their organization.

The most important information on Nicholson's screens was the line that compared the actual number of volunteers with the number the model had predicted they would get. With no counterattack at all, four hundred people should have volunteered by the end of the day; with the opposition fighting them every step of the way, they would be doing well if they ended the day with the two hundred volunteers Nicholson had predicted. And they would be in a vulnerable position even if they hit two hundred. Hill's party workers could keep working on their volunteers over the next day or two and a lot of them would give in to the pressure and drift away before they were completely committed. His plans were based on the assumption they were going to pull off another prank and give the public another emotional jolt. If he canceled the second prank, there would be an error of unknown size in all his calculations.

A light flashed on the console. He turned off a lecture in the middle of a sentence and Sue came in on his phone screen and flashed him the hand signal that meant she had been talking to Peggy Dazella.

"I've got a question from Operator X," Sue said. "I told it how things look and it wanted to know if we expect to go ahead on schedule."

"I'm still trying to make up my mind. Is X still interested?"

"It says it's still willing but it's not sure about some of its colleagues. It said it needs to know pretty soon."

"It may not be working with all the colleagues it thought it would?"

"Right."

"How many colleagues does it expect to have?"

"It says it may be fifty percent short."

Nicholson covered his emotions with a frown. He glanced at the figures on the console and shook his head.

"They've had some second thoughts," Sue said. "X didn't sound too happy, either."

"Did it tell you when it needs to know?"

"It sounded pretty anxious."

"Ask it if it can give me until after supper. I shouldn't make up my mind before I watch the numbers during prime time."

"Do you have any idea how you'll decide?"

"I have a feeling it's going to be negative. Don't tell X I said that, but that's the way it looks now."

"The numbers look that good?"

"I'll talk about it when I get home."

The tally was four volunteers behind the prediction when he left the office at four-thirty. He checked it again as soon as he got home and by then it was five behind.

Sue stood beside him in the bedroom and watched his face darken. She squeezed his hand and he patted her on the back and shook his head.

"I wouldn't be worried about it if I wasn't worried

133

about Mead," Nicholson said. "I'm afraid he'll back out on us if we pull off a second prank and he sees the results on the news again."

"X didn't look very happy about it, either. It's willing to go back tonight, but it said it probably wouldn't have volunteered to do this if it had seen the results first."

"And X is a hell of a lot tougher than Mead is."

"If I'd had to listen to him for five more minutes today. . . ."

"I noticed you looked a little taut when you got through with that rehearsal."

"He can't make one Goddamned move without telling you what a great strain it is for him to do this and how much he wishes he didn't have to dirty up his precious little soul."

"I thought you handled it very well. I'm probably the only person in the world who would have realized he was annoying you."

"Doesn't he think the rest of us have some feelings about this, too?"

"He probably thinks we're some kind of moral monsters. He can agree somebody has to do something like this, but he's not sure a really moral, upright person *could* do it."

"And now you're afraid you may have to put the whole project in danger just because you've got a prig for a candidate."

Nicholson shrugged. "I knew he'd be a lot of trouble to work with when I decided to go ahead with him. He bothers me almost as much as he bothers you, love. But we couldn't have gotten another candidate before the primary if I'd had the biggest war chest I've ever dreamed of."

"Can you still put an organization together if you don't let X go ahead with the second item on the program?"

"We'll be in a weaker position than we should be if we don't do it. We can still form an organization if we try to go ahead without doing it. But I can't guarantee the organization will be as big as I've been hoping it would be."

"And you won't know if it's big enough until we add up the tally at the end of the first stage and see if we've succeeded?"

"Right."

"He said he was willing to do it, didn't he?"

"He could also get a great deal of pleasure out of telling us to go to hell and giving up his great political ambitions because he's too moral and virtuous to do the kind of rotten things we're doing. He'll probably get a lot less squeamish once we get him committed. But right now he's got to be handled like he's made out of glass."

"Thank God I don't have to spend as much time with him as you do."

"He isn't exactly the kind of man you and I would pick for a friend. Do you know what our trusty machine's serving up for supper yet?"

"I decided we'd better change the program and have a buffet. I told the girls we're having a family Christmas party."

A yellow bulb lit up above Mead's button on the console. Nicholson tapped the button and Mead's head and shoulders filled the phone screen.

"I thought I'd see how we're doing," Mead said. "How's it look now?"

"It looks like we're beginning to feel the effects of their efforts. We just picked up our twenty-first volunteer. The machine claims we would have gotten twenty-six by now if they hadn't been working against us."

"So we lost about a third of the people we should have picked up since two-thirty?"

"We should have gained nineteen and we gained fourteen instead."

"And you still think you can pick up two hundred?"

"It depends on how things go after supper. We've only made a relatively small number of calls so far. The results could still be random."

"Does it look like we're going to need the reinforcement we talked about?"

"I'm still thinking about it. I'm still hoping we can

avoid it but we won't know for sure until we get the count during prime time."

"It looks like I may as well relax then. I'll be home all evening but I think I'd rather not ge disturbed between eight and nine if you can avoid it. This is a big time of the year for ballet loonies."

"I'll probably know how we're going to do by nine. You can call us any time you want a report."

They signed off and Nicholson glanced at his watch.

"I wish I knew what he was thinking," Sue said.

"I think I'll see if I can give our charming daughters a little fatherly companionship between now and dinnertime. Do you think there's any chance the Big Four may be willing to play a game like Fish with their father?"

"You'd better try a little roughhousing with Ellen and Nancy first. I've been sitting in here most of the day and I think they're beginning to show the effects."

"You may as well come out of hiding, too."

"I've been working on some second thoughts for the stuff for the trucks. I think I can finish it up if I can slip in some more time at the console before dinner."

He hung his jacket in the closet and stepped into the hall. Ellen ran down the hall like a two-year-old professional athlete and he dropped to one knee and swung her above his head. Nancy slouched against the wall at the end of the corridor and watched her younger sister with the tolerant smile of a girl who had already decided she would rather have daddy come to her.

Christmas was a special season in the Nicholson household. It was the only time of year the whole family spent two consecutive weeks under the same roof. His nine year old, Rachel, had come home from Nigeria in early July, and one of the girls had been attending a camp or taking advantage of a "growth opportunity" all through the rest of the summer. And his eight year old, Margaret, had headed for an experimental art school in Germany as soon as the summer had ended. Bright children could hop around like business executives nowadays, if their parents would let them, and he had decided it would probably be good for them. Their rank in the family lineup changed constantly; every girl got to be the oldest child in the house now and then, and there was no danger Margaret and Lorin would get lost in the middle of the crowd. Sooner or later every child got to be the only child in the house for awhile.

He checked the tally at eight-thirty and discovered it was now eighty volunteers behind the unadjusted prediction. They would have recruited three hundred and fifty two volunteers if Hill hadn't been fighting back. They had actually recruited one hundred and seventy one.

The computer had already called most of the people they could hope to reach. He would be lucky if they pulled in the two hundred volunteers he had promised Mead.

He sat down at the console and gave the computer a string of instructions. Figures started crawling across two screens.

Fifty percent of the people who had volunteered had been the Gruber types he had expected; they were already typed in the model or they had responded to a hidden test when they had called up and volunteered. The other fifty percent were listed under "type unknown." He had assumed the unknowns would be the same types as the knowns and he had asked the computer for a prediction in two different situations: with the second prank and without it.

The first prank had aroused a strong reaction in the people he was trying to attract. The reaction wouldn't last without reinforcement, however, and Hill could speed up the rate at which it decayed. If he omitted the second prank, Hill would keep pulling recruits away from them at the present rate. They would lose twenty to forty percent of their recruits within the next twenty-four hours. They would be lucky if they finished the second day with one hundred and forty volunteers.

If he told Peggy to go ahead with the second prank, on the other hand, the situation would improve right away. They would pick up some new recruits and most of the current recruits would resist Hill's efforts. They would finish the second day with a minimum of one hundred and ninety-five volunteers.

Sue slipped through the door and dropped into the chair beside him. The computer handled all of the housework and most of the routine child care women had handled when he had been a boy, but his wife still collapsed like an exhausted mother as soon as she put the girls to bed.

"How's it look now?" Sue said.

"We're going to have to work like hell if we don't do something that will reinforce the first stimulus."

"We'll have to let X know pretty soon. We can't keep it standing by much longer."

"I'm almost certain we'll lose Mead if we do it. The closer I get to a decision, the surer I get."

"And they're really hitting us that hard?"

"They've got the manpower and they've got all the information they need to use it without wasting motion. They're operating on an open field where they can see everything and we're operating in a fog."

Mead's light lit up on the console. Nicholson's eyes widened.

"It looks like he got impatient," Sue said.

Nicholson tapped the button. Mead jumped onto the phone screen. "We just go a three-minute intermission," Mead said. "How's it look now?"

"I'm afraid we're doing a little worse than I thought we would. It looks like we're going to finish up the evening with a hundred and seventy to a hundred and ninety volunteers."

"Is that significant?"

"It depends on what it means in the long run. I'm playing around with the computer now."

"How about the reinforcement? Have you checked that out yet?"

"I'm still trying to make up my mind. I don't want to do it if we can possibly get along without it. But it looks like it's going to be a borderline case."

"Have you come up with any estimates of the kind of risk we'll be running if we don't do it?"

Nicholson hesitated. He didn't want to scare Mead off but there might be some advantage in telling him the risks were pretty big. A man like Mead would probably be a hell of a lot happier if he thought he was taking a big risk for the sake of a moral principle.

"We'll probably go into the next phase of the operation with a big handicap," Nicholson said. "We'll have to work our heads off."

"But it looks like we can still form an organization?"

"If we work our heads off. If we make sure we don't miss a trick."

"I'd rather not do it if we can avoid it."

"I'm checking it out as closely as I can. We won't do it if we don't need it."

"I'd rather not do something like that if it looks like there's a good chance we can get along without it. I'd hate to have us lose this thing after all the hell you've been through, Ralph. This is no time to get squeamish if we really need another stunt like that. But I don't think we should do something like that again if we aren't sure it's necessary. I'd rather run a bigger risk and work a little harder."

"That's about how I feel. I just wanted to make sure we know exactly what the risks are before we make a decision."

Mead glanced at something on his right. "How long do you think it'll be before you can give me an estimate?"

"It'll probably take about twenty minutes."

"I'll call you as soon as the show's over. They're starting the last act now."

"Have fun."

The phone screen blanked. Nicholson slumped back in his chair and stared at the numbers on the information screens.

"It looks like you were right on target," Sue said.

"It's going to be a real handicap. I wasn't kidding him."

"I wonder if he'd bo so Goddamned moralistic if he had a child of his own growing up in this mess."

"You may as well go ahead and tell X it's off. I'll finish up the stuff I'm working on now and we can take another look at the stuff you've been developing for the trucks. Maybe we can put our heads together and come up with some propaganda that'll reduce the damage."

XV

Reporters had been pestering Mead since he had made his first statement. Six local TV stations had hit him with phone calls as soon as Dr. Zellman had replied to the statement. A hover car from Boyd's personal TV station had raced down the canal and a reporter had tried to get inside the gate with a camera and a microphone. Mead had stuck to the script Nicholson had given him, however, and had insisted he wasn't going to answer the sheriff until he had given the matter some more thought.

"I don't believe in shooting from the hip," Mead said. "This is an important issue. I don't believe in making public statements until I've had a chance to think them through and say exactly what I want to say."

"Does that mean you may be reconsidering your previous position, Dr. Mead?"

"I gave the statement I made this afternoon all the thought I could give it. I've been thinking about doing something like this for several months. I called up several knowledgeable people this morning and listened to their opinions before I decided to go ahead and commit myself. I'll be just as careful when I make my next public statement."

His delivery was a little pompous, but Nicholson nodded anyway. Mead was supposed to be a prudent, self-controlled, authoritarian leader. He would repel thousands of people, but thousands of others would think he was just the man they were looking for.

At ten o'clock the next morning, Mead went back on television and recited a statement Sue had written for him. One hundred and thirty citizens had told him they wanted to join the organization he was forming, and he could assure every citizen of Windham County that none of his volunteers were the kind of people who would join a "vigilante" group. They were all peace-loving, ordinary, public-spirited people who were willing to give up some of their time to help their neighbors sleep soundly. He didn't want any other kind of person in the organization. He could understand why many intelligent citizens were worried about this development, however, and he had therefore decided he should organize a public meeting for everybody who had volunteered or who was thinking of volunteering. The meeting would take place at eight P.M. that evening at the Pembroke shopping center. Every citizen who wanted to volunteer was invited to come out and show his neighbors that Dr. Zellman was making a big mistake when he called them vigilantes.

Three automatic trucks started maneuvering across the county as soon as Mead went off the air. Programs prepared by Nicholson's computer guided them toward areas where their propaganda would have the maximum effect. The lead truck pulled up to the first stop on the list and Sue settled down in front of her console and watched her work make its first appearance in public.

A giant castle filled the air above the truck. Hordes of furry barbarians flowed up the walls on ladders. A Charlemagnish king stood on top of the castle wall and drove the barbarians back with kicks and blows, and an occasional spanking with the flat of his sword. The first spectators stepped in front of the camera that was trained on the area around the truck, and Sue started relaxing. It was a cold day and she had been telling herself she would be doing well if she got half the people who seemed to be coming out.

Nicholson came in on the conference hookup and picked up the truck on his own screens. "It looks like we're off to a good start anyway."

"I hope so," Sue said.

A number on the right-hand corner of the screen told her one hundred and thirty-five adults would probably be home within a block of that particular stop at that particular time. At least fifty adults were already standing in front of the truck and more people were joining them. They knew they were going to be sold something but she had put together a come-on that had made them put on their jackets and tumble into the cold anyway.

"It's a good come-on," Nicholson said.

"It looks like it's mostly a male crowd, too. I'd say the adult males make up about sixty percent of the crowd."

She had always hated people who used terms like "adult males" and "adult females" when they were talking about people. But she always found herself using them when she did advertising work.

Four more screens lit up on her console. The other two trucks had reached their first stops.

The animator on the first truck started projecting the next part of the cycle. A big, muscle-bound moron strutted onto the center of the stage with his arms raised and his head thrown back. A dozen barbarians climbed on top of each other and made a ladder with their bowed bodies. The moron climbed up the ladder body by body and the audience smiled as he showed off his muscles, while the king waited for him with his sword arm hanging casually by his side.

A barbarian wizard waved his hand across a huge fire and sent a flock of black hawks flying toward the king. Barbarian acrobats tumbled and somersaulted on the left side of the truck. Golden lights blinked on and off along the bottom of the truck and announced Mead's meeting as if they were announcing the top Hollywood superspectacular extravaganza of 1955. The advertisement was a good-humored spectacle which was supposed to amuse children under ten and create a pleasant, neighborly mood in the rest of the audience, and it looked like it was having the right effect. Most of the kids in the audience were laughing and pointing. Most of the adults looked like they were glad the truck was broadcasting something that entertained their children. Their houses were crammed with TV screens and entertainment gadgets, but giant, three-dimensional cartoons were still relatively novel.

She didn't understand all the mathematical theorizing behind her husband's schemes, but she knew the organization was supposed to attract three types of recruits: people who needed social status; people who felt hemmed in and restrained by society; and people who disliked children and young people and felt guilty about it. And she knew it was supposed to be especially attractive to people who had repressed these emotions, or who didn't know how strong their emotions were. For people like that, the organization would be a tremendous release. They would satisfy their emotional needs. They would build up their status, strike out at organized society, attack children and young people; and they would still have the feeling they were good, upright individuals who were obeying their moral codes and protecting society. If she made an appeal to their emotions that was too open and obvious, however, they would begin to understand their real motives, and the experience would become turbulent and disturbing. Everything that happened to them had to be surrounded with a glow of pleasure that would make the organization a happy, tranquil experience.

"Does it look very funny to you?" Sue said.

"After all the times I've seen it? It looks like they're reacting the way we hoped they would."

"It might look a little droller if I made the big guy a little fatter. Why don't I try it on one of the trucks and see how they like it?"

"It sounds fine to me."

She leaned back in her chair and gave the computer a string of instructions. Computer-controlled animators were expensive gadgets, but they had an advantage which had made them the basic tool of the psych writer: a single writer could sit at a console and create a complete animated cartoon without a staff of animators. The animator had a huge library of programs and the writer could pull a basic image out of the file and modify it until he got the exact picture he wanted and modify it again as soon as he started getting feedback from his audience. The big guy would be a little fatter the next time one of the trucks made a stop and she could shrink him again right away if she decided the extra weight had been a mistake.

Mead came in on the conference call and watched the screens without saying anything. The children laughed at another piece of slapstick and Sue glanced at Mead and noticed he was smiling.

The cycle lasted four minutes and twenty-seven seconds. The air around the trucks was electrically heated and the odor generators on the truck were releasing odors that suggested a pleasant, cozy environment: the smell of chestnuts over an open fire, a little hint of wood smoke, the odor of clothes that had been dampened in the snow, and other odors that had been tested by advertising agencies and commercial psychologists, and that could be bought off the shelves of a dozen companies. No one could guarantee they would make a particular individual feel relaxed, but they would relax seventy percent of the people in the audience, and the effect would help set the mood for the whole group.

"It looks like we're doing something people like anyway," Mead said.

"They came running out as soon as they saw it," Nicholson said.

The king's image stretched two feet higher. He waved his hands over the scene and the barbarians halted their attack and started turning cartwheels on the castle green and tumbling and somersaulting off high, quivering human towers. Hawks swooped along the castle wall like feathered stunt planes. Trumpeters appeared on the walls and long streams of shining light leaped out of their instruments. Fireworks soared above the castle. The entire image swelled until it towered a hundred feet above the audience. It shattered like a bubble, a kaleidoscope of color flowing out of the sides, and a blue dirigible floated above the crowd with the king waving out of a basket slung underneath.

Big gold letters flashed on the side of the dirigible. Golden mechanical arms reached out of the truck and started handing out blue and yellow invitations to Mead's meeting. The truck crept away from the corner with the king waving from the dirigible, and the dirigible started shrinking as if it was vanishing into the distance.

Sue studied the three crowds as the trucks pulled away. Most of the younger kids were waving good-bye at the king. A few men were glancing at the meeting notices and sticking them in their pockets. Nobody looked angry or annoyed.

"It looks like you did a great job," Nicholson said.

"I don't see anybody shaking his fist."

"You're sure you gave them enough advertising about the meeting?" Mead said.

"That's one of the things we're keeping an eye on," Sue said. "There's a phone number on the meeting notice. We're going to watch the phone count and see if we need more copy."

Nicholson glanced at the screen that was supposed to tell him the number of information calls coming in. The first tally appeared on the screen and he set his face. Three people had phoned in for information and received a replay of Mead's announcement of the meeting. Five or six would have called if he had let Peggy go ahead with the second prank.

"It still seems like a crazy way to do things," Mead said. "I'm certain you know what you're doing. But I'd still like to get out there and give the sons of bitches hell."

The tally on Nicholson's console changed again. Ten people had phoned in for information instead of the twenty they would have picked up if he had let Peggy pull off the second prank. Mead and Sue could see the tally on their screens, too, but he was the only one there who knew it would have been twice as high if he hadn't called off the second prank.

"It's the results that count," Nicholson said. "It seems like a crazy way to do things to me, too, sometimes."

XVI

Peggy Dazella had collected twelve volunteers from her dojo gang. They met Nicholson in a hotel suite in downtown Philadelphia and he handed out their equip-

145

ment and explained their assignments to them. Four of them would carry spy devices he could use to observe the crowd from inside. The rest would be human stimuli he could use to manipulate the crowd; role players who would follow the orders that came to them over the phones hidden in their ears.

Peggy's friend Harry had done most of the actual recruiting again and it looked like he had done a good job under the circumstances. The volunteers didn't know the real reason they were doing this, but they were being paid three hundred dollars for the evening and that was all the motivation they needed. They were the same kind of people who had participated in the prank and they were used to living in a society in which you could pick up some extra money by acting as a puppet for some organization that was trying to bamboozle the public.

They were still young people in their teens and early twenties, however, and nobody that age was completely happy working with the party in power. They all looked a lot more enthusiastic when he told them they were going to help him disrupt one of the biggest political organizations in the country. That kind of sabotage job would have appealed to him when he had been their age, too.

The human gauges were a harder problem. The gauges had to have the same personality structure as the people who were supposed to attend the meeting—and people like that didn't spy on the public merely because they wanted to have an adventure or make a little easy money. The employment service he had called had been certain it could come up with six men who had the right profiles; its staff had been very surprised when they had only found four men who met the requirements and who were willing to take the job.

"I did my best for you, Dr. Nicholson," the man at the employment service had said. "You can try another company if you aren't satisfied, but we did everything we could. I called thirty-five people before I got these four for you."

"That's fine," Nicholson said. "That's about what I expected."

The gauges wouldn't know they were acting as gauges, of course. He had told the employment service they were going to be spying on the audience at the meeting and he had pretended they were going to be helping him with a psychological experiment. And he kept up the pretense after they were sitting in the hotel suite.

"Basically, we're collecting data on how people react to certain kinds of speeches. All you have to do is wear this equipment under your jackets and move around according to any instructions you get over your earphones. Most of the time you'll be wandering around the crowd at will."

The equipment had been laid out on a long coffee table. The four men stared at it as if they had just been told they were supposed to eat it.

"This is the first time I've ever let anybody talk me into doing something like this," a big, gray-haired man said. "I wouldn't come near it with a hundred-foot pole if my daughter didn't need the money."

"I'd appreciate it if you'd put the stuff on now and let me test it out," Nicholson said. "It'll only take a few minutes and I'd like to make sure it's working right."

The four men slipped out of their jackets and buckled the equipment harnesses over their shirts. Nicholson switched on a portable console and four blinking lights advised him all the circuits in the harnesses were working.

"I'd better tell you a little bit about the meeting you're going to while we're at it," Nicholson said. "It's a recruiting meeting for a citizens volunteer group that's going to be patrolling the streets in Windham County. Did any of you see that stuff on TV about the prank some kids played there yesterday?"

Blinking lights informed him the monitors had recorded a change in each man's blood pressure. Instruments located directly over their chests had picked up the changes that had taken place in heartbeat and respiration. Tiny sensors scattered over the harnesses were

147

measuring the heat that emanated from each man's body and the slight chemical changes that took place in the air around his skin as his sweat varied.

"You mean the little bastards that recorded private conversations and broadcast them all over the damned county?"

"I wouldn't exactly call that a prank."

"This citizens' patrol organization grew directly out of that incident," Nicholson said. "The man who's organizing the group decided it was about time he did something about stuff like that.

"And he's willing to let you spy on the people who'll be there?"

"He didn't want to do it when we first asked him about it, but he changed his mind when we made it clear this is a noncommercial project and none of the information we're picking up will tell us anything about individuals. Did everybody here actually see the scenes they showed on TV?"

His finger brushed a button that would place a mark beside this point on the record. He had a level for them when they were relatively calm and now he would have a level for them when they were thinking about something upsetting.

"I saw them all right," the gray-haired man said.

The other three nodded. "They were all over the TV when I got up that morning," the tallest man said.

"A lot of the people there feel pretty upset about this," Nicholson said. "Please make sure they don't observe you."

"We'll be lucky if they don't lynch us. If my daughter didn't need the money—"

"Nobody will suspect you're observing them if you're reasonably careful. Now if you'll turn on your cameras, please, and aim them right at me. . . ."

Mead was going to have a very pleasant time at the meeting. The crowd was going to be small, but it was going to give him the kind of experience that made politicians feel like they were floating in a sea of love and approval.

He ate a quick dinner in a restaurant near his office and arrived at the Pembroke shopping center at six P.M. The command truck he had ordered was already parked near the meeting area. The catering crew had roped off a section of the park and started setting up tables and stringing colored lights.

Two knots of people were standing around the meeting area watching the caterers work. A big, busy crowd was circulating through the stores around the park. A couple of hundred people were strolling under the trees in bulky, woolly looking leisure clothes. Bursts of music and whiffs of odors were drifting across the park from the advertisements in the stores.

He introduced himself to the caterer and walked across the meeting area with the caterer by his side. The entire twenty-acre shopping complex had been domed over and the park was as warm as a pleasantly chilly evening in early autumn. The people who came to the meeting would be surrounded by Christmas crowds and October weather.

"It's too bad you don't have some live music," the caterer said. "This would have been a great setting for a medieval ensemble."

Nicholson stopped in front of the button rack and checked out the layout. The wires that connected the rack with the truck had been carefully concealed in a tangle of wires from the lights. The buttons for the status seekers were clustered in the upper left-hand corner. *Don't take it lying down* and *Give the cancers hell* were down in the lower right-hand corner. The rest of the buttons had been scattered over the rack in a pattern that looked like it matched the chart he had given the caterer—*Protect our children* intermingled with *A free society is an orderly society. Support your community* mixed in with *Keep our children safe.*

The portable bar had been set up in the back of the meeting area, ten feet from the ropes. All the drinks listed above the dispenser were the mild happy drinks he had ordered.

Mead stepped around the group of people standing at the back of the meeting area. He maneuvered his heavy body over the rope fence and Nicholson stepped up to him and held out his hand.

"It looks like things are moving right along," Mead said. "How's it going?"

"So far it looks like we're right on schedule."

"It looks like they're setting it up just the way you wanted it. How'd we do on the final results on the stuff you did with the trucks?"

"I checked the tally just before I left the office. We would have done better if we'd stuck with our original plan but right now it looks like we'll still be okay."

"I hope to hell we draw a good crowd. I haven't been this tense before a speech in ten years."

A heavy vehicle hummed down the street that connected the park with the entrance to the dome. Nicholson glanced over his shoulder and saw a big truck slowing down behind his command truck. The back of the truck edged around and the automatic pilot started guiding it into a parking place.

"We seem to have some company," Nicholson said.

Mead turned his head. The truck was unmarked but the top was studded with lights and antennae.

"I guess they decided to pay us a visit after all," Mead said.

The front of the truck maneuvered into the parking place. The wheels straightened out and the guidance system eased it forward and shut off the motor ten feet from the back of Nicholson's truck.

"That's a big truck for somebody who's just observing," Mead said.

Nicholson shrugged. He had told Mead the opposition might try to interfere with the meeting and he had assured him they would be in a strong position if anybody tried anything. Crowd manipulation was a tricky business when you were working against opposition. He wouldn't have tried it himself if he had been in Hill's position and he had made a few plans just in case Hill didn't agree with him.

"We're still in a good position if they try anything," Nicholson said. "We don't have as many volunteers as I'd hoped we'd have by this time, but we're still in a good position."

Soft music started flowing out of the loudspeakers

on Nicholson's truck. Mead tipped his head to one side and listened.

"It sounds like we'll have a good sound system anyway," Mead said.

"I got the best one I could get."

"I just hope my speech sounds as good as the music."

"You'll probably have everybody eating out of your hand as soon as you start talking."

"And you'll stand there and fight it out with the opposition toe to toe if they try to start anything."

A taxi pulled up behind the new truck. The back door swung open and a man jumped out. John Hill waved at them jauntily and trotted up the steps on the back of his truck.

Nicholson's hand floated away from his side. He smiled at Hill and waved back.

Mead glanced at Nicholson out of the corner of his eye. He turned back to the people who had started strolling through the entrance and Nicholson looked over the area as if he was giving it another inspection.

"There's nothing like chivalry" Mead said.

"We'll see how much the little cancer smiles when we're done."

"I hope so."

Three young men had just strolled through the entrance. A dozen more people were standing around the button rack and the happy drink bar. The three young men waved and Mead waved back.

"It looks like it's time I started mixing with the customers," Mead said.

"I'll see you later," Nicholson said. "Good luck."

"Have fun."

Mead stepped toward the crowd with his hand out and a friendly, pleasant smile on his face. More people were filing out of the subway stop across the street from the park. A scattered, strung out crowd was flowing toward the meeting area through the trees.

The back door of the truck opened as Nicholson climbed the steps. It clicked shut behind him and he sat down at the console and activated the TV cameras that were trained on the meeting area. A bank of screens lit up in front of him and he looked over the camera angles and made some adjustments.

He pressed the red button that put him in touch with Mead. "This is Ralph, Al. Can you hear me all right?"

Mead waved at the truck over somebody's head and made the V sign.

"That's fine," Nicholson said. "Thanks a lot."

He checked out the screens that were connected to the button rack and glanced over the tally. Eleven people had picked up buttons so far. Five of them had picked up *Protect our Children.* The rest were evenly divided between *Support Your Community* and *Keep Our Children Safe.*

Peggy Dazella and her boyfriend stepped into the roped off area. Mead stepped up to them with his hand out and Nicholson switched on Peggy's circuit and listened in while they shook hands with Mead and gave him the names they were using.

"We saw your truck when it came through our neighborhood today," Harry said. "It's about time somebody did something like this."

"I just hope we get enough people out," Mead said.

"I'll be pretty disappointed if we don't get a good response," Peggy said. "We've been needing some leadership on this issue for a long time."

Four more people filed through the entrance. Mead turned toward them with his hand out and Peggy and Harry wandered over to the bar and started selecting drinks.

"This is your friendly voice from nowhere," Nicholson said. "Nod if you can hear me."

Peggy's blonde head bobbed once.

"That's fine," Nicholson said. "You did a good job there at the entrance. Can you help me out while I run a test?"

Peggy nodded again.

"I'm going to test the air currents in here. I checked them out before I told them where to park the truck but I think I'd better do it again. You should get a whiff of an odor in a moment. Say something to each other with the word in it that fits the odor."

He reached for the controls of the odor generator and punched the buttons that would release the smell of onions. Peggy and Harry eyed each other across their drinks and studied the people coming through the entrance.

Peggy's nose wrinkled. "I really did feel like having onions with that steak we had tonight. I would have done it if we hadn't been working here."

"We all have to make some sacrifice for society," Harry said. "Even onions."

"Thanks a lot," Nicholson said. "We're all set."

Peggy and Harry strolled over to the button rack and picked out the two slogans he had told them to choose. A panel on the left side of his console advised him his four human gauges were all present and broadcasting information. People were coming through the entrance in a steady stream now and he could see more of them coming toward the area. His role players were drifting through the entrance in twos and threes and screens were automatically lighting up and giving him a view from inside the crowd as they came in. The music switched to something sprightly and gay and Mead wandered through the crowd shaking hands and keeping up the pleasant, amiable manner Nicholson had told him he should assume.

The back door swung open. Sue stepped inside the truck and he nodded at her and turned back to the flood of information coming at him from the console. He could shut most of it out and concentrate on one thing if he had to, but he had learned you had to watch everything as much as you could. His brain was integrating a mosaic of information. Every detail could count.

"How's it going?" Sue said.

"He's doing fine so far. He's got his doubts but he's sticking with the script."

The role players were giving Mead the little signals that were supposed to make him feel everything was going fine. The clumps of people milling around the meeting area looked like they contained more than a hundred people altogether. The tally from the button rack indicated they were getting the kind of people they had been trying to attract.

"I see we've got some neighbors," Sue said.

"Junior himself."

She stopped behind her chair. He glanced at her out of the corner of his eye and saw her hands twitch.

"He waved at me when he stepped out of his taxi," Nicholson said.

"I thought I smelled something sick when I was coming across the park."

A band of dim red light crept across the meeting area. A warning light blinked on a screen on Nicholson's left. A band of dim blue light moved across the crowd like a cold shadow.

Nicholson glanced at the screens that showed him Hill's truck. Four lights had lit up on the roof and started turning.

The band of red light moved across the crowd again. The cold blue shadow slid after it. Red swept around again.

He flipped a switch and gave the computer a string of instructions. He glanced at a screen crowded with symbols and a yellow line advised him there had already been a definite increase in the rate at which the noise level was climbing. The instruments attached to his human gauges had already picked up a fifteen percent increase in the body movement count.

Red and green lights played over the fountain behind the roped off area. The music on the loudspeakers started moving at a faster tempo. The caterer's lights winked on and off in a complicated pattern that included the red and blue bands and integrated the bands and the fountain in a low-keyed prelude to a lawn party. The yellow line leveled off and started climbing at its normal rate. The body movement count reached a peak and started dropping.

Sue dropped into her chair. She slipped on her headset and pulled a pen out of a container.

A yellow light glowed on top of Hill's truck. A sensor detected it at once and the computer made another change in the lights. He had given it the numbers that described the kind of pattern he wanted and the computer would now treat the pattern as an equilibrium which had to be restored every time it was interrupted. The results wouldn't be as good as they would have been if Hill had left him alone, but they would probably do.

Two of Mead's personal friends opened a bin in the bottom of the truck and rolled a portable tally counter across the grass. The people in the front of the meeting area turned around and watched them and one of the men held up his arms and shouted for attention. Anybody who wanted to join the organization could walk up to the tally counter and give it his name, address and thumb print. Mead had set up an account for the organization and the volunteer's dues would be transferred to the account as soon as he pressed his thumb against the thumb plate. The computer would correlate his name with any information it had about him and the accuracy of Nicholson's model would go up one more notch.

"I wonder how many role players our friend has out there," Sue said.

"I'm deducting twenty from all the totals."

Six men had stepped up to the tally counter and formed a line. Most of the people in the area had turned back to their drinks or gone on wandering around the area with drinks in their hands.

One hundred and thirty people were now milling around the meeting area. At least thirty of them were standing by themselves.

He pressed the button that activated Mead's earphone. "This is Ralph, Al. I can see a lot of people standing around by themselves. Can you have some of your friends strike up conversations with them?"

Mead was standing in front of the bar with two young rocks and a fashionably dressed woman who looked like she was old enough to be their mother. He tugged his earlobe without taking his eyes off the woman and Nicholson cut off his earphone and pressed the button that connected him with all his role players simultaneously. He didn't want to start the formal meeting until he had a bigger crowd, but the people who were standing by themselves would probably begin to feel uncomfortable if he let them stand around too long. He had seen people like that at every political meeting he had attended during the last ten years. Political organizations always attracted people who were lonely or who had trouble making friends.

Half the people in the crowd had picked up buttons so far. Sixty percent of them had picked out the slogan that indicated they felt frustrated and hemmed in by society. Thirty percent were supposed to be people who were angry at kids. Ten percent were looking for status.

"Computer: record crowd now on screen. Match faces with records. Advise number persons classified each Gruber type."

A table appeared on the screen directly in front of him. Twenty percent of the faces in the crowd could be matched with faces in the files and given a definite classification. Forty percent belonged to G types that should probably be included in the frustrated group. Twenty percent belonged to miscellaneous types. The rest could be evenly divided among the other types he was trying to attract.

Nicholson shook his head. By now Hill probably knew the exact Gruber type of seventy percent of the people in the crowd. Every face in the entire Goddamned county was probably filed in Hill's computer.

Mead's cronies had started striking up conversations with the people who had been standing by themselves. Peggy Dazella had pulled in four men at once and she looked like she was treating each one as if she thought he was the greatest man she'd ever met. People were beginning to check their watches and wonder when the meeting was going to start.

He glanced at the clock. It was seven-forty. He had about a hundred and eighty people in the crowd.

"I think you should go on in five more minutes, Al. You can start spreading the word."

Mead pulled his ear again. He looked around as if he was estimating the size of the crowd.

Nicholson pressed another button. A mobile speaker's platform rolled away from the truck and took up a position near the tally counter. People started breaking up their conversations and moving toward the platform.

Mead squared his shoulders and started toward the platform. The role players and some of his friends cheered him on and he waved at them with the self-mocking air that apparently fitted his attitude toward speechmaking.

Nicholson stared at the tallies on his screens. He hesitated and then he pressed Mead's button.

"Try to keep it humorous, Al. Play up the stuff on the dangers of lawlessness and the importance of order. Use about half the stuff on kids but try to keep it lighthearted. Use a little of the stuff in section three but don't worry if you have to leave it out. The numbers indicate it'll be all right if you just sprinkle a little of that stuff through the rest of the speech."

The computer changed the lighting to a warmer, darker pattern. Nicholson pressed a pair of buttons on his odor generator and a soft odor drifted through the crowd. No one there could have identified it, but it was an odor guaranteed to calm any audience that was primarily male; a synthetic mixture that exactly duplicated the odor of a woman's breast. It would only last a couple of seconds before the generator automatically switched to a neutral odor but that would be enough. He had used it at a political meeting at which half the people in the audience had been women and it had still brought the meeting to order faster than any technique he knew.

Mead waved at a couple of well-wishers as he climbed up the steps of the shiny white platform. A woman yelled at him as he settled behind the platform and he waved back at her and switched on the mike. His voice drifted across the crowd at the conversational level Nicholson had recommended.

The noise level dropped as soon as Mead started talking. The human gauges had calmed down as soon as the odor had touched them. Nicholson's mikes could pick up murmured comments here and there but most of the people in the audience were paying attention.

The crowd chuckled at one of the jokes Sue had written into the script. Nicholson glanced at the screen that showed him the area in front of the speaker's platform and saw Peggy Dazella looking up at Mead and smiling at his jokes as if they were both sharing a wonderful evening and she approved of every word he was saying.

XVII

THE EQUIPMENT hidden on his spies relayed a montage of faces and voices. The role players scattered through the audience laughed and nodded and murmured their support. Hundreds of emotional signals were reaching the man on the platform and the man in the truck was watching the screens and noting all the evidence that he was reacting to them.

"It looks like he's really starting to bubble," Sue said.

Nicholson nodded. He had told Sue he wanted her to be funny without ridiculing the cops and the sheriff and she had put together a speech that made Mead sound like a professional comic. She had attacked the weakness of the county police system and appealed to the prejudices of the people who were angry at the kids, and she had done it without saying one nasty word about anyone.

"You really did a great job," Nicholson said. "It's nice to work with a real pro."

"It's your secret weapon. One clever, amoral wife."

He picked up the bitter note in her voice and reached out and squeezed her hand. Nobody could sit in the control room in a crowd situation without feeling either power drunk or a little disgusted with himself.

Heads turned toward the right-hand side of the roped in area. Mead glanced over his shoulder and stopped in the middle of a sentence.

Nicholson switched on the camera mounted on top of the truck. Four big hover cars had driven up and parked behind Hill's truck. A couple of dozen young people in their teens and early twenties were climbing out of the cars and strolling toward the meeting area.

Spotlights swung back and forth on the hoods of the cars. The lights around the meeting area responded to a new pattern and then changed again. Red and blue lights swept across the faces of the people in the crowd. The detectors on the human gauges picked up the first signs of tension and anxiety. Emotional voices reached him through the mikes planted on his spies.

What's going on now?

I should have known we'd have trouble.

Can't the little cancers even let us have a Goddamned meeting?

It looks like we may have some fun after all, Arnie.

Nicholson's hands leaped across his console. "Keep looking at Mead, Peggy. Look at him like he's the only guy who could possibly know how to handle this."

"Keep on with the speech another few seconds, Al. Try to look like you're in perfect command of the situation. I don't know what these little bastards want but we've got plenty of artillery in the arsenal if they start making trouble."

"Role players. Keep calm. Keep your attention focused on Mead. Act like you're looking to him for leadership. Try to counteract anybody who starts acting up."

Mead turned back to the crowd and continued his speech. Peggy Dazella looked up at him with her face glowing with confidence. Sue switched on her headset and started feeding the role players lines.

The newcomers were strolling along one side of the meeting area and lining up along the rope. Silver statues of the goddess of death glittered on the chains around their necks. The loudspeakers built into their clothes surrounded them with a halo of the quiet, off key music that had become popular during the last couple of years.

They folded their arms over their chests and stared at the people on the other side of the rope. They stood there without moving and the people in the meeting area eyed them uneasily. A few men were edging toward the opposite side of the meeting area. There was a steady rise in the number of comments Nicholson could hear over his mikes.

"Tell them something like you see we have visitors," Nicholson said. "Be as noncommittal as possible. Get back to your speech as soon as you can. Don't threaten them but don't act like you're giving in to them either."

Mead looked down on the kaligang as if he were a Roman consul looking down on a mob. "I see we have visitors," Mead said. "I guess our meeting notices got around."

A woman's voice broke through the comments on the side of the crowd near the kalis. "I should have known the bugs would come crawling out of the cellar. They look like they're the same little cancers that nearly gave my poor husband's poor mother a heart attack last week."

Heads nodded. A man muttered something that sounded angry and the people near him nodded in agreement. A big, barrel-chested kalirock stuck his thumbs in his belt and smiled at the woman across the rope.

"I'll bet your husband wishes we'd gotten our hands on him, too, madame. He can probably use a few weeks in the hospital after chewing on a piece of meat like you for twenty years."

"There must be something wrong with the temperature control system in here," a girl kali said. "I do believe I can see half the men here shivering every time I look at them."

A tall, blonde girl tossed her head back and looked down her nose at the crowd. "It must be wonderful to be a hero. I have a feeling I could put every one of them on the ground with one of my arms in a cast."

"I wouldn't count on it," the other girl said. "You might need two hands for some of them."

"Remember the time we put that shopkeeper on the ground and put his wife to work in front of him? I'll bet he'd never seen his wife do that before."

Two human gauges were pouring moisture into the air at a rate that had gone up twenty percent in the last four minutes. Three microphones were transmitting heartbeats that had taken a sudden jump and leveled off ten to fifteen beats above normal.

"I think you'd better drop the speech, Al. Turn up the volume and see if you can drown the kalis out. Try to keep everybody calm. I think Hill sent the kalis here to provoke a riot. The best approach will be to tell the audience the kalis came here to make us look bad and now's our chance to show the public we aren't a bunch of vigilantes. Don't let a bunch of troublemakers interfere with us and wreck the one thing they're really afraid of. We'll call the police right away. Tell the audience somebody in your organization's doing it. I don't know if they'll come or not but it may buy us some time."

"Role players—try to keep people calm. They're probably trying to provoke a riot. Keep an eye on anybody who looks like he's trying to stir up trouble from inside the crowd. People follow the people around them in this kind of situation. Give them an example that'll keep things quiet."

Hill knew the kind of people they were trying to attract. He knew how they would feel afterward if he could get some of them to start slugging. They had come here looking for a compromise with their emotions and the man in the other truck was trying to ambush them with the violence and anger that stalked them everywhere they went.

The blonde kaligirl was pointing her finger at a tall, matronly woman who was standing near the edge of the crowd. "I really think I'd rather try that one myself. She looks like she may have had some experience at that kind of thing."

The man standing beside the woman stiffened. He started to step forward and the woman put her hand on his arm.

Nicholson stabbed the record button on his console. Kalis were making comments like that up and down the line and most of the people they were gesturing at looked like they were responding. Hill could point his role players right at the people who would react to that kind of stimulus and tell them the exact approach they should use.

Mead was looking down at the kalis as if he was made out of rock. Peggy Dazella nodded approvingly as his voice boomed over the meeting area. Approving comments reached Nicholson from the mikes hidden in the crowd. The people on the right-hand side of the meeting area followed Mead's advice and started edging away from the kalis. A few people were still slipping out of the entrance but most of the people in the crowd looked like they were keeping their emotions under control.

A voice rose out of the crowd. A well-dressed, middle-aged man had cupped his hands over his mouth and stepped out of a knot of people in the back of the meeting area.

"And what are we supposed to do while we're waiting for the cops to get here, Dr. Mead? Hand over our wives so these little bastards can maul them in public?"

"I'm glad you feel like eating this kind of thing, Mead."

"Would you let that blonde disease talk to your wife like that?"

Nicholson sagged back in his chair and studied the screens as if he was studying a game board. Hecklers were yelling at Mead from every section of the crowd but they all sounded isolated. None of the people around them seemed to be giving them any support. Most of the comments he could pick up were coming from people who were agreeing with Mead.

Hill had brought in some strong artillery but he was attacking a tough position, too. Most of the people in the crowd were reacting as if they were the kind of people he had tried to attract, as if they were so afraid of violent emotions they had surrounded them with twenty-foot walls and an arsenal of defensive responses.

The human gauges were still tense but the numbers on their readout had peaked just before Mead had started talking and they were all on their way down.

"Hold your ground, Al. You're doing fine. The people doing the yelling are primarily role players from Boyd's organization. We brought in the kind of people we wanted and they aren't the kind of people who get stirred up easily. He's putting a lot of pressure on them, but right now it looks like you can ignore the hecklers and move on to the next stage."

Mead's voice blared over the loudspeakers again. Hecklers shouted at him from the crowd but he raised the volume another notch and pushed on. Kalis were still pointing at people and making comments but most of the people in the meeting area were ignoring them. Most of the people Nicholson could see looked like they were annoyed at the hecklers.

He jerked his thumb at the bank of buttons in front of his wife. "You'd better take charge of the role players, Susan. They're doing all right so far but we'd better have somebody keep a close watch on them. They could ruin everything if they got carried away and wrecked the tone of this thing."

Sue switched on her headset and pushed in a button. A woman started screaming at the kalis from the side of the crowd and Mead ignored her and pointed at the tally counter.

"We're going to start our first patrol as soon as this meeting ends," Mead boomed. "Our first volunteers will be watching the streets tonight. Anybody who wants to help us with this project can step up to the counter right now and sign up. I'll be right down here in front if you've got any questions. You can talk to me or you can talk to any of the people with the green buttons in their lapels. We've got some good stuff in the bar and it'll be open for the rest of the evening. I'm sorry we're having problems with uninvited guests but I hope you'll go ahead and have a good time anyway."

He stepped off the platform and Nicholson's role players waved and clapped on cue. Most of the crowd joined in the applause.

The kalis leaned against the trees and watched the crowd with sardonic, knowing smiles. Hands toyed with the little statues hanging on their chests. The tall, blonde girl squatted at the base of a tree and tugged at the grass.

"Role players. Everybody except three and four move up to the counter and sign up. Three and four, move to the back of the area when the dance music comes on and start dancing. One and two, try to stay on the side near the kalis after you sign up. Keep an eye on them while you're working. The rest of you circulate and talk the thing up. Join the groups around the men with the green buttons. Try to keep the conversations going."

Peggy and Harry joined the handful of people at the tally counter. The rest of the role players fell in with them and the line swelled until it was about twenty-five people long. The brightest dance music in the files floated out of the loudspeakers and a redheaded girl and her boyfriend started dancing near the bar.

Three more people joined the line in front of the counter. The crowd at the bar thickened. People started walking around the meeting area with fresh drinks in their hands. Half a dozen people had left the area when Mead had finished talking but most of the people in the audience had stuck around.

You just have to grit your teeth and put up with it. You'll see Santa Claus and every reindeer left in Alaska before you see any cops around here. Those bastards in the Goddamned TV studios are probably watching every move we're making right now. I don't care what those morons in Mead's church think, if that blonde disease starts moving in on me like that, she'll get everything these young animals deserve.

Thirty-seven people had signed up since the meeting had begun. Five people were still standing in line in front of the counter.

"I think you'd better give them another speech, Al. We'll give them about two more minutes to get adjusted to the kalis and then I think you'd better get back to the platform and urge them to sign up."

The leader of the kaligang pushed himself away from the trees and looked around the crowd. His hand toyed with his statue. He jerked his head and the blonde girl and two kalirocks stepped away from the tree and fell in beside him.

The leader stepped across the rope. He stopped just inside the meeting area and heads started turning all over the crowd.

The blonde girl stepped across the rope and started

moving toward the woman she had insulted earlier. The music coming out of the loudspeakers in the kalis' clothes became more discordant and irritating. The leader and the two rocks sauntered toward the people they had picked out in the crowd.

The numbers coming in from the gauges shot up again. A woman screamed an insult at the blonde girl. The role players who had been heckling Mead raised their voices again.

"Where the hell are your cops now, Mead?"

"What are you going to do now? Make a phone call?"

"Get 'em out of here! Get the little cancers out of here!"

Nicholson's left hand jumped to Mead's button. Sue straightened up in her chair and he stretched out his arm and covered her hand. His voice was as flat and businesslike as the voice of an astronaut who had just discovered a meteor had destroyed half his oxygen supply.

"Don't say a word for another minute or two, Al. Look them over like you're taking it all in and thinking things over. We're still pretty certain they aren't going to hurt anybody. They may get pretty rough verbally but they probably won't strike the first blow. I'm getting a good picture of the crowd's reactions. I'd like to see how this develops before we make another move."

"Role players, keep up the same line. Try to get between the kalis in the crowd and the rest of the people. Keep looking calm, but be ready to move if you get the word. We'll have to move in fast if any violence develops and stop it with the minimum amount of fuss."

Peggy and Harry stepped in front of a cluster of people. A man started to move toward one of the kalirocks and Peggy put her hand on his arm.

The kalileader's side men stopped in front of a young girl and her boyfriend. They looked the girl over and the boy put his hand on the girl's shoulder and watched them warily.

"I wonder how good she is with her mouth," one of the rocks said. "I'll bet she'd be pretty good."

"Maybe she and her boyfriend would like to give us a demonstration."

The boy stiffened. The two kalis grinned and inched toward him.

The blonde girl stepped in front of the woman she had insulted before. She said something inaudible and the man who was standing beside the woman stepped in front of her with his fists clenched. The girl tipped her head back and laughed soundlessly.

"It looks like it's time you got back on the speaker's platform, Al. Use the same type of approach you've been using. Tell them anybody who wants to volunteer can line up in front of the tally counter. Everybody who doesn't want to volunteer should go home. We're sorry we have to cut the evening short but nobody should have to put up with this kind of thing. We'll only be playing into their hands if we let anything happen. We can't stop the kind of harassment we're putting up with tonight but we all know they don't have the guts to do anything violent when anybody's watching."

Mead moved toward the platform through a chorus of comments. The two side men turned away from the couple they had been harassing and closed in on a young man who had been standing by himself.

Nicholson pressed Peggy Dazella's button and gave her another order. Mead looked over the meeting area with his big hands gripping the edge of the speaker's platform and his voice boomed over the crowd once more. A couple of dozen people started moving toward the tally counter as soon as he told them they had to make up their minds right away.

Peggy Dazella jumped in front of the counter and threw up her arms. Her long hair tossed and glittered around her shoulders.

"Let's fall in line everybody! Let's show the cancers they can't scare us into running away! The people we're trying to control are standing right in front of us. Now's the time to stand up and be counted."

"You're really playing this one by ear," Sue said.

"It's the only way we can do it," Nicholson said. "We don't have the kind of detailed information Hill's working with but I'm pretty certain I'm making the right moves."

Most of the people in the crowd were moving toward the counter. Some of the people who had already signed up had raised their voices and started urging the others on. The four kalis were still strutting around the meeting area but most of the people Nicholson could see were flowing past them as if they didn't exist.

"Move the platform toward the center of the area, Al. Place yourself between the kalis and the line in front of the tally counter. You're getting a great response. Try to treat it like it's something really significant, like they're doing something they'll really be proud of when they think about it later on. The kalis came here to make you look bad and instead everybody's falling into line and showing the little bastards the united front they'll be facing in the future."

The speaker's platform moved forward. Mead's voice boomed again. Peggy Dazella raised her fist above her head and a third of the people in the line followed her lead.

"A great moment in the history of American civilization," Sue said. "Decency triumphs again."

Nicholson patted her hand without taking his eyes off the screens. The four kalis inside the meeting area were inching toward Mead's platform. The rest of the gang had left the darkness under the trees and moved up to the rope.

"You'd better move in closer to the line," Nicholson said. "Don't give the kalis a chance to surround you."

Mead twisted the controls and moved his chariot closer to his troops. Twenty more people had registered at the tally counter. The people who had already registered were hovering around the head of the line and watching the kalis.

The kalis jumped over the ropes and ran toward the line shouting war cries. Panicky voices screamed all over the meeting area. Everybody in the line stepped back as if somebody had given an order. Hill's role players raised an angry shout. Half a dozen people stepped toward the kalis.

The kalis stopped ten feet from the line and broke into laughter. The men who had been backing toward the exit straightened up and looked foolish. The kalis broke up their formation and started sauntering along the line making comments.

A man stepped out of the line. He ran toward the tall, blonde girl at top speed and his fist swung out. His knuckles crashed into the girl's face. Drops of blood glittered under the lights. The girl swerved away from him and dropped to her knees with her hand over her mouth.

Two more men ran out of the line. Scattered voices yelled. Wild, confusing bands of color swept across the area. A blinking light on Nicholson's console warned him the spy equipment had picked up a gas. A display on one of the screens advised him it was an anti-inhibitive gas.

Twenty percent of the people in the line moved toward the kaligang. A kaligirl knelt beside the blonde girl and screamed insults at the crowd. The rocks in the kaligang stepped back and looked around them with the confused faces of people who had suddenly set off something bigger than they had expected.

Nicholson rose out of his chair. His finger stabbed at a button on the left side of his console. A heavy sedative gas spewed out of the nozzles along the side of the truck.

"Role players, get the leaders in the kaligang! Use your hypnotics! Get them under control with the minimum amount of violence. Don't let it look like you're leading an attack on them."

The dojo gang moved out like a trained army, their nervous systems protected from the sedative by the same membrane Hill's role players were wearing in their nostrils. Hands slipped inside jackets and came out with injectors hidden in their palms. Peggy Dazella flowed toward the leader of the kaligang and the big rock hesitated with his hands half raised. He dropped into an unarmed on guard in the last split second before Peggy closed in and Peggy slipped past a kick at her shins and twisted his hand behind his back. Her hand slipped inside his jacket.

The two gases drifted into the park ventilation system. The kalis who were still free shouted insults at the dazed people standing in the line. Mead looked down at the madhouse beneath him as if he was wondering if he should throw up his arms and start screaming imprecations at the mind masters of Babylon.

Five kalis were staring into space with role players from Peggy's dojo gang standing beside them. A plump, motherly looking woman had stepped into the space between the crowd and the kalis and started urging people on.

"Role players. Tell your hypnos to stay quiet. Tell them to start backing out of the area. Walk off with them as if you're leading some drunks."

"Al. Start thanking the people in the crowd for keeping their heads. Act like nobody made a move toward the kalis. One man lost his head out there but everybody else stood there like rocks. They're throwing a lot of stuff at us but we're still doing all right. I only saw about twenty percent of the people actually start forward myself. Start signing them up again. See if we can get them back on the track."

The reading coming in from the gauges indicated they were almost out of their stupor. They would hear Mead thanking them for their self-control as their emotions returned to normal and in another five minutes most of them would probably have accepted his description of their actions. The gas was colorless and odorless and its main effect should have been a sudden, stupefied heaviness, followed by lethargy. He couldn't use it very often, but most people would accept a comforting explanation of their own actions when they were faced with something unexplainable. They had gone through a sudden emotional storm that had been so intense most of them would have trouble remembering what had happened, and Hill was handicapped by the fact that most of the people in the crowd didn't *want* to know they were capable of violence.

Sirens screamed in the distance. Nicholson swung a camera around the scene and saw a line of policemen running across the park. Two police cars were pulling up behind his truck with their sirens dying and their red lights flashing.

His hands danced over the switches that put him in touch with Mead and the role players. The policemen, who were approaching the area on foot, stopped ten feet outside the rope. Mead moved his platform forward and stopped between the crowd and the police.

A police captain jumped out of his car and ran across the grass. He took up a position in front of his men, and the big kalirock standing beside Peggy stepped forward on cue and held out his hands with his palms up.

"It's all right, coppies. We're all right. Some of our rocks lost their heads a little but it's all right. We'll be out of here before you know it, coppy."

A hypnoed kaligirl stepped away from her puppet master and inched toward the police captain as if she was ready to fall on her stomach as soon as he raised his hand. "We were just popping around, Captain Brackett. We were just popping around and it got a little out of hand. You aren't going to rough us up just because we were popping around, are you?"

The big, blonde girl lurched to her feet with her hand over her face. A kalirock grabbed her shoulders and she pointed at the people in the line.

"They nearly ruined my Goddamned face, Brackett. I've got blood drying all over my face. Why don't you rough up some of these nice, fat, middle-aged carcasses for once in your life, *captain?*"

The police captain looked over the crowd as if he was studying the situation. There were thirty men behind him and they were standing in a solid line with their riot shields on their left arms and their electric stunners in their hands.

The captain turned away from the hypnotized kalirock whining in front of him and pointed at the blonde girl. He was a big, handsome man and Nicholson knew he was the most controversial cop in the county. The cop haters in the area always referred to the police as "Brackett's boys."

"What happened to you, miss? You claim somebody hit you?"

"I didn't even see him coming. He ran at me out of the crowd. The next thing I knew he'd hit me in the face and I was lying on the grass with all this blood on my face."

"She brought it on herself, Brackett! She was talking to us like we were garbage."

"We were holding a peaceful meeting and these little cancers came marching up here and started strutting around like they thought they could walk all over us."

"We were holding a peaceful, legally authorized meeting," Mead said. "They came here and tried to provoke us into violence and we called your headquarters and asked for protection, Captain Brackett. That girl and some of the people with her were walking around saying things you wouldn't say to a dog and everybody here was keeping himself under control. One of the men here finally lost his head and ran out and hit her before anybody could stop him. Every other person here kept his head and stayed right where he was."

Brackett looked over the crowd again. His handsome head turned from side to side as if he was positioning it under a bank of spotlights.

"Who hit you, miss? Can you point the man out?"

The girl's finger moved across the crowd. It hesitated for a long moment and then it stabbed at a man who was standing near the back end of the line. Her voice rose hysterically.

"It's him! It's the one! I only got a glimpse of him before he hit me but that's him."

The man she was pointing at looked around him as if he thought she was pointing at somebody near him. Three cops moved forward and poised behind their captain.

A fat, middle-aged man stepped out of the crowd. He stared at the man who had been accused and his head snapped back as if he was doing a double take on the stage.

"She's lying through her teeth, Captain Brackett. I saw the character that hit her with my own eyes. He

171

weighed thirty pounds more than that man does and he must have been four inches taller."

"If you trust that little cancer, Brackett, you're even dumber than people think you are."

"She'd accuse her own mother if she thought you'd rough her up while she watched."

Angry mutterings ran through the crowd. The man who had been fingered stepped back and looked around him as if he was hunting for an exit. Nicholson checked his human gauges and saw the tension reading climbing toward the ceiling again.

Brackett gestured at the three cops standing behind him and they moved forward and fanned out. Three more cops fell into place beside him and eyed the man who had been accused. A couple of people had closed in around the man as if they were trying to protect him but the man made no attempt to defend himself.

The three cops moved into the crowd and started asking people questions. Every person they approached stiffened as they came toward him.

The fat man was still pleading with Brackett. "The guy that hit her must be ten blocks away from here by now, Captain Brackett. He's walking away from here scot-free and everybody knows it."

Brackett stared at the man as if he was looking down on a yapping animal. He was a head taller than ninety percent of the people in the park and his shoulders looked like they would have absorbed the blows of grown men as if they had been shrugging off the blows of children.

"We're checking the lady's story right now, sir," Brackett said. "Why don't you relax and let us get things straight?"

"The guy that hit her left as soon as he did it. I saw him run away myself."

Nicholson scanned the montage on his console. Mead was looking down at the crowd as if he was taking in every word and planning his next move. Give him ninety more seconds without definite instructions and he would probably start feeling like an idiot and try to act on his own.

A girl ran out of the crowd and jumped on the

fountain behind the bar. She balanced on the rim of the fountain with the water rising behind her and her voice shrieked out of a hand-held public address system.

"They're going to run him in for nothing! The little blonde's got Brackett wrapped around her finger. They're going to take him down to the station and work him over while she watches. She doesn't care who they get! She'll stand there and watch and they'll do anything she tells them to!"

The girl's voice rose and fell in a mad singsong. Her black hair was flowing around her shoulders and she was talking with the crazy incoherence he had seen in certain kinds of patients. She was either drugged or she was one of those not very bright people who grab the chance to get some public attention and start making wild statements in public—or a good actress who had studied the kind of person she was trying to imitate. He had seen lonely, aging women walking down the street muttering curses at their husbands and families, and they had sounded exactly like the wild-haired creature balancing on the edge of the fountain.

Brackett flicked his fingers at his men. Four cops stepped out of line and moved toward the fountain at a trot.

A young man ran out of the crowd and grabbed one of the cops by the shoulder. Three more men ran out of the crowd and dropped into unarmed on guard positions between the cops and the fountain.

Lights and music rose toward another climax. Another blast of anti-inhibitive gas polluted the atmosphere. Half the people in the crowd surged toward the four cops.

The girl danced up and down on the platform. Voices screamed. Mead turned around on the speaker's platform and stared at the truck as if he thought Nicholson was going to throw up the side panels and fire a broadcast.

Nicholson pressed the button that released the sedative. He shouted an order at Peggy and her role players and the dojo gang moved away from their

173

prisoners and started interfering with the people who were trying to get at the cops. The sedative spread across the area and the people in the crowd started slowing down and staring into space as if their IQ's had suddenly dropped forty points.

The police plowed into the three role players who had stepped between them and the girl. Electric prods leaped in and out. The girl hopped up and down in front of the fountain and begged people to help her. The three role players fell back and the police shook them off and trotted toward the fountain.

Sue rose out of her chair. Mead threw up his hands and shouted something at the role players who were urging the people on. Brackett gestured with his hand and two police stepped out of the line and started moving toward the crowd.

Nicholson gulped in a long breath and reached for Mead's button. Every word he uttered had to give Mead the impression he was absolutely certain he was making the right move. Every gram of panic had to be squeezed out of his voice.

"I just gave them another dose of the sedative, Al. I can't do it too many times but one more time won't hurt us. I think you'd better tell them the whole group will go to the station with the cops and make sure they don't hurt anybody. Give them a moment to come out of the sedative and then start talking. Tell them anybody who wants to come with you can and everybody else should go home. He's aroused some pretty strong reactions but we can still control things if we can channel their emotions into something legal. He'll probably try to build them up again but he'll have trouble doing it if we can get them channeled into something else."

Sue's eyes widened. He patted her hand and she dropped into her chair and stared at his face. His brain had pounced at the first idea that had flashed across his consciousness and now he had to push ahead with it and hope he had made the right move. The computer had spoken. Every move he was making had been calculated by an expert who was using all the resources of modern psychology. Mead could listen to the calm voice in his ear and be certain he was in the hands of knowledgeable, competent people who were guiding him toward victory.

Dazed faces were staring at the scene through the confusion created by chemicals and by conflicting assaults on their emotions. A lot of people had rushed at the police but Peggy and her gang had managed to hold them back before anybody had actually reached the cops and started fighting with them.

Brackett gave his men an order. More cops moved forward. The girl jumped off the fountain and two policemen chased her through the spray and grabbed her arms.

The cops stepped toward the crowd and faced it with their electric stunners poised. They were glaring at the crowd as if they were hoping somebody would hop out of the line and give them a chance to knock a few heads in, but they were obviously staying inside a carefully chosen limit. Nobody could possibly claim they had been doing anything wrong when they had gone after the girl. She had been inciting to riot and Brackett had told her to shut up, and anybody who looked back on this tomorrow would know Brackett had been right.

The girl struggled with the two policemen. A big hand twisted her arm behind her back and she shrieked like a punctured animal.

"Help me! Somebody help me!"

Nicholson glanced at the reading from his human gauges. "Start talking to them now, Al. Make it sound like a real event."

He flipped Peggy's switch and the role players started drifting through the crowd, giving Mead support. Sue started feeding them lines and giving them directions and he rested his hand on Mead's button and studied the screens. A few people were moving away from the edge of the crowd but most of the people on the screens were turning toward the voice blaring at them over the shoulders of the police.

The microphones hidden in the crowd picked up confused questions. The girl shrieked again and the two

175

cops picked her up by her elbows and started carrying her across the front of the crowd.

The girl twisted and heaved in the policemen's arms. "Help me! Why won't you help me?"

A couple of Hill's role players moved forward. The police raised their stunners again and the role players looked around them and paused when they realized nobody was following them.

"We'll be waiting for her when she gets to the police station," Mead blared. "My lawyers'll be there, too. No one is going to hurt her. She's going to get the same kind of honest, fair treatment every citizen in this country has a right to."

The girl shrieked again. The door of the police car slammed shut behind her rump. Nicholson slumped back in his chair and clutched Sue's hand.

XVIII

Sue picked out some music that would have sounded good at a carnival and put it on the truck's speaker system. The blue dirigible she had used in the afternoon rose above the truck with the barbarian wizard, the muscle-bound moron and the king, all clowning in the basket. A couple of Peggy's people started singing and Nicholson thought for a moment and then told them they could go ahead as long as the singing was individual and spontaneous.

"Stick to carnival songs," Nicholson said. "Don't sing anything that sounds political. Don't give people the impression they're engaging in mass singing that's being coordinated by the leadership."

The people he had attracted were essentially private people. They would start rebelling as soon as they began to feel they were being manipulated with oratory and singing and the other techniques mass movements had used throughout history.

The big air lock in the side of the dome opened ahead of the parade. Mead drove through the doors on his speaker's platform and the people lined up behind him reached for the controls on their clothes and turned up their heaters. Twenty people changed their minds about the walk and hurried back inside. Some of them claimed they were going to ride the subway to the police station, but most of them were obviously going to drop out before they got there.

Sue dipped the dirigible as the truck followed the crowd through the doors. Faces peered at them out of the cars moving down the opposite lane. The moron leaned out of the dirigible and waved and Nicholson saw a couple of kids wave back at him out of the window of a car.

Hill's truck crept through the doors and followed them down the street with all its extra lights turned off. Mead turned left at the first stop light and the parade turned the corner after him and followed him down the canyon between two long walls of seven-story and eight-story apartment houses. Shadows appeared in the windows along the street. Scattered individuals stepped out of the main entrances of the apartment houses. The dirigible swung back and forth between the buildings on both sides of the street and Sue's three characters waved at the people on the balconies as they floated past.

Two police cars fell in behind Hill's truck with their red lights flashing. Three motorcycle cops roared around the corner in front of the line and stopped in the middle of the street.

Mead held up his hand and stopped the platform. The crowd pulled up behind him with the usual amount of hustling and questioning, and one of the cops gunned his motorcycle closer to the platform.

"Try to keep up the same front," Nicholson murmured. "We aren't trying to obstruct the police and we aren't afraid of them either."

The cop leaned back on his motorcycle and looked up. He waited for Mead to say something and Mead looked down at him and waited for him to speak first.

"I knew they'd start harassing us," a man said. "If we aren't living in a Goddamned police state, I don't know what the hell this is."

"I'm afraid I have to advise you you're leading a parade down a main street," the cop said. "You can't have a parade without a permit."

"We're walking to the police station together," Mead said. "There's a lot of us but we're just walking to the police station together. We aren't having a parade."

"You're walking down the middle of the street blocking traffic. You can't do that without a permit."

The other two motorcycle cops were eyeing the people in the line. Their eyes would rest on a particular individual for several seconds at a time and then they would move on to somebody else.

"Ask him what he wants you to do," Nicholson said.

"What would you like us to do, officer?"

"You can't go marching down the middle of the street blocking traffic. You'll have to get up on the sidewalk."

"Go ahead and do what he wants. They may have something unexpected hidden up their sleeve, but it looks like they're probably just trying to make everybody feel angrier."

Mead turned around on the platform and gave the crowd the word. They moved onto the sidewalk without making too many comments and Nicholson moved the truck forward and took up a position beside the center of the line. Mead waved his hand again and the crowd moved forward.

"Why don't you see if you can find somebody who looks like he needs a lift?" Nicholson said. "Pick out a young girl if you can. Or somebody elderly and respectable. Get as many people up there as you can fit on that thing. It's only a little thing but it could have a good effect on the crowd."

Mead cruised down the line and picked up a young girl and a man who looked like he might be in his early sixties. A few people waved at him and made comments about the girl as he rode by and Mead picked up Nicholson's advice and smiled back.

The motorcycle cops were gunning their motors and following the crowd along the side of the street as if they were keeping a herd of cattle bunched together. The numbers coming in from the human gauges were still trying to climb off the top of the chart. Some of the people in the crowd looked like they were pushing themselves across the Sahara without water.

"We'd better work fast when we get to the station, Al. Have some of the people get inside the station right away. Get the rest of them started on their patrols. Don't let them start wandering around wondering what they're supposed to do."

A couple of people started belting out a new song and about thirty percent of the crowd beside the truck joined in. Sue gave the computer some instructions and the barbarian wizard leaned over the side of the dirigible and waved his arms as if he was conducting a chorus.

"I hope to hell it works," Nicholson said. "I grabbed the first idea that came into my head and started us moving."

"I don't see what else you could have done."

"He had me in a corner. I got us out of it but we're still a lot more vulnerable than we were."

"He must have twenty role players out there. And he's got all those cops and kalis working for him, too."

"He probably has ninety percent of the people in that crowd classified. I've got a good picture of the crowd as a whole, but he can pinpoint particular people and lean on them right where they're weak. He knows exactly how they'll react and I have to work with probabilities."

"And you still think we can come out of this mess on top?"

Nicholson shrugged. He had lived with Sue a long time and he knew she wouldn't ask questions like that if she wasn't thoroughly discouraged. She had worked beside him for the last two hours without bothering him with questions and she would be doing her best not to disturb him now that he had indicated he wanted to talk for a minute. If he multiplied the emotion she was expressing by a factor of five, he would probably have a good picture of the emotions she was actually feeling.

"It depends on what he does next. I'm trying to keep things calm but he's using the cops to keep up the pressure on them. He probably even told the bastards exactly who they should look at while they were talking to Mead. They won't be able to put their fingers on it tomorrow, but right now a third of the men in that line are probably mad at the cops."

"He must have a Goddamned army out there."

The crowd stopped in front of the dome that covered the main square of Pembroke. The big door slid open and they marched in with Mead in the front and two trucks tagging along behind. Mead turned the platform toward the park in the center of the dome and they marched across the grass toward the old-fashioned glass and steel courthouse on the other side.

A police car came down the street and stopped in front of the courthouse. Two policemen climbed out of the car with the girl between them.

Nicholson's eyes darted across his screens and charts. The police car should have been moving five times as fast as the marchers. The girl should have been standing inside the courthouse minutes before they reached the park.

The girl threw herself against a cop's shoulder and started thrashing. She screamed for help and two men broke out of the crowd and started running toward her. Five police cars hummed around the corner and pulled up in front of the courthouse.

The girl's knee rammed into a cop's testicles. He doubled over and the girl wrenched herself away from the other cop and broke into a run. She sprinted across the street toward the crowd and five more men stepped out of the crowd and ran toward her. They fell in around her with the other two men and the police piled out of their cars and lined up in the middle of the street.

The girl turned toward the crowd and held out her hands. Her high, wild voice rose above the park. "Save me! For God's sake, somebody help me! They beat me up in the car! They tried to rape me right in the car! They said they'd shoot me full of drugs and make me do anything they want me to do!"

Tired, defeated voices muttered curses. Faces looked up at Mead and waited for directions. Nicholson glanced at Sue out of the corner of his eye and saw her hands gripping the edge of the console.

He pushed Mead's button without hesitating. His voice sounded as firm and confident as the voice of a computer simulation that had been programmed to sound like a therapist who was absolutely certain his patient should take his advice.

"Try to do exactly what I tell you, Al. It's a tricky situation and we have to play it just right. Put yourself between the cops and the people. Tell them to stay where they are and wait until you can send somebody inside with the girl. Tell them the girl's hysterical and you'll have somebody with her every step of the way."

Mead pressed a control. The platform hummed across the grass and he swung it around and stopped with his back to the girl. He held out his hand and most of the people who had been moving forward stopped where they were.

"Help me!" the girl screamed. "Please help me!"

Brackett took up a position in front of his men. His voice boomed out of the loudspeaker on his belt.

"This girl is a legitimate prisoner. Anybody who interferes with my men is going to find himself sitting in a cell."

"Stay where you are," Mead blared. "Stand fast. Nobody's going to hurt this girl as long as we're here. We'll stay here all night if we have to."

"They won't let you go in the back room! They'll slip me a drug when they're supposed to be checking me in! Don't make me go in there! Don't make me let them get their hands on me!"

"She can't be more than twenty years old," a man said.

"They'll do anything they want to once they get her inside that hell hole. There isn't one damn thing we can do to stop them."

"They'll get her inside and then they'll laugh in our faces."

Brackett's men moved forward half a step. Half the people in the crowd moved toward them.

"Stand your ground," Nicholson said. "You're the authority figure. You can hold them back if you don't let them see you waver. It isn't a sure thing but the odds are all on our side. They *want* you to hold them back."

Mead raised his fist above his head. The crowd stopped as soon as he started talking and the girl and her five bodyguards ran around the platform and stopped between Mead and the crowd.

Brackett and his cops took another step forward. A man in the crowd shook his fist at Mead and told him to go back to the old lady's home and masturbate.

"You're a damn fool if you think you can control those cops, Mead. They'll do anything they feel like with her."

"They'll fill her full of drugs and she won't even know they did it."

"How would you like to put on a skirt and go inside there in her place, Mead?"

The girl pulled at the ripped cloth above her left breast. She pointed at a bruise and half the men in the line moved forward.

"I've got black and blue marks up and down my whole damned body! They spent the whole ride working me over."

"Don't back down," Nicholson said. "Keep them in line. They want you to keep them in line."

Mead raised his fist again. "We're going to take our prisoner," Brackett blared. "Tell your people to back up, Mead. Have them back up at least a hundred feet."

Mead hesitated with his fist poised above his head. Angry, confused faces watched him from the crowd.

"Go ahead and ignore him, Al. Keep on talking. You'll probably have to back up sooner or later but you can ignore him for the moment."

The girl and her seven buddies moved closer to the front of the crowd. Nicholson gave Peggy and her gang a new set of orders and they started moving toward the platform. "This is no time to take the law into our own hands," Mead said. "I know what they could have done to this girl already. I've lived in this county as long as most of the people here. But that doesn't give us an excuse to act like a lynch mob, either. We're here to help the law, not break it. The cops don't want an organization like this any more than the kalis do."

The girl stretched out her arms and stepped toward the crowd. Her face was haggard and sweaty and there was a dark bruise on her left cheek.

"You aren't going to help me by sending a damned

182

committee in there! You're the only hope I've got. They'll come after me as soon as I start to run. I can't get away if you won't stop them."

"And what'll you do if you do get away?" Mead said. "Grab the next ship for the moon?"

"They won't come after me if I get away. My lawyer'll keep me out of jail. They'll have to cross state lines to get me."

"They'll kill her in there, Mead. They'll wreck her for life."

"It's the only thing we can do for her."

"What kind of people do you think we are, Mead?"

The girl inched closer to the crowd. A dozen people edged away from the crowd in the back.

A big, middle-aged man shouldered his way out of the crowd and marched up to the girl. Nicholson had noticed him before but up until now the man had been watching the whole uproar in almost complete silence. He had been standing off to one side with a couple of friends, and he had been watching everything that happened with shrewd, alert curiosity of a detective or a good reporter.

The man held up his hands. The police inched forward another step. Somebody in the crowd asked the man what the hell *he* wanted.

"I've heard enough," the man said. "I don't know about you people, but I've heard everything a reasonable man has to hear. We can look at this girl and see the evidence with our own eyes. The police roughed her up in the car and they'll rough her up again as soon as they get her inside. Albert Mead is a decent, well-meaning man but we aren't going to do one damned bit of good once they get their hands on her. They'll slam the door in our faces and we'll stand there looking like idiots. We all know they can hold us up for just thirty seconds and slip a drug in her. I don't know who this girl is but I've got a daughter her age myself. I'm not going to stand here and let her get roughed up just because Dr. Mead is afraid we'll get a bad image on TV."

"This is your last warning," Brackett boomed. "We're

183

going to move in. Are you going to back up or do I have to let my men fight their way in?"

Nicholson's eyes scanned his screens. The middle-aged man had been standing there like a piece of camouflaged artillery. Hill had waved his wand and the crowd had been given an authority figure who sanctioned their violence, a solid, respectable, reasonable man who told them they could let loose just this once and let the world have it. They would hate themselves tomorrow but tonight they would feel respectable and righteous right up to the moment they felt the cops' electric shocks banging through their bodies.

The police moved forward at a slow walk. Somebody in the crowd yelled for action and most of the people in the front ranks took a hesitant step forward. The middle-aged man put his hand on the girl's shoulder and she looked back at the cops and shivered like a frightened animal.

"The real criminals here are the police, if you ask me," the man said. "It's time the respectable people in this county stood up for themselves."

"Go after the girl," Nicholson said. "Grab her yourself. Don't hesitate. Get her under control and get her on the platform."

Mead straightened up. Sue swung around in her chair and stared at her husband's face.

"Don't hesitate," Nicholson said. "Don't let anybody stop you. Push them out of your way if you have to. Make them run. Get the girl in your custody."

Mead twisted the controls of the platform. He shot toward the girl and the men standing around her turned toward him and threw up their hands. Mouths dropped open. Mead yelled like a cossack and they realized he wasn't going to stop and jumped out of the way.

The girl stumbled away from the platform and plunged at the front of the crowd with her head lowered. The police broke into a run. Voices rose all over the park.

"Go get her," Nicholson said. "Show them who's boss. Kick them out of the way if you have to."

Hands grabbed at Mead's platform. The girl ran into the crowd and the yelling, cursing man on the plat-

184

form forced his way toward her. "Get out of my way, Goddamnit! I said we'd do this legal and I meant it. Get out of my way!"

"Get her before the police get her," Nicholson said. "Don't let the police get their hands on her."

Sue rose out of her chair. The girl broke out of the side of the crowd and started running toward the exit. The girl looked like she was running away, but she was running along a path that would put her in the hands of the police a hundred yards before she reached the exit.

Mead broke out of the crowd and raced toward her. He hummed up behind her and the girl looked back over her shoulder and swerved toward the cops. The platform shot past her and Mead twisted the controls and tried to come around.

"Don't let the cops get her," Nicholson said. "Take her prisoner yourself. Take command. Show them you can take command."

Sue's hand flew to her mouth. "Ralph. *Ralph.*"

Mead bore down on the girl again. Three role players jumped in his way and then scattered when he kept on coming. Brackett yelled an order through his loudspeaker and the cops picked up their pace.

The girl swerved to the right. Mead jumped off the platform, as if he was bulldogging a steer, and leaped toward her. The girl screamed and he jumped at her again and grabbed her by the shoulders. He twisted her arm behind her back and she screamed again.

The platform had stopped twenty feet away. Mead pushed her toward it as the cops closed in on him and made her climb up the steps. A cop pulled out his pistol and Mead backed up the platform and put a good fifty feet between him and the cops.

"Don't let them bluff you," Nicholson said. "They won't shoot. Keep the girl in your custody. Don't let them take her until you've got a committee all picked out and ready to go in with her."

Sue shook her head. The police stopped running and Mead looked down at them from his platform.

"Tell them you said this would be a legal organization," Nicholson said. "Tell them we aren't going to take anything off the cops and we aren't going to break the law either."

The girl moved. Mead did something with her arm and her face twisted with pain.

"I said this would be a legal organization, ladies and gentlemen," Mead said. "I said we'd work with the law, not against it. This girl is going to get a fair hearing in there. We aren't going to take one damned thing off any cop in this county but we aren't going to let some scatterbrained girl lead us into breaking the law either. If you can't obey the law, keep the hell away from this organization."

"Hand that girl down," Brackett boomed. "You're holding a legal prisoner. Hand her down at once."

"Point out the people you want for volunteers. Keep on exerting your leadership. Pick anybody that looks like he'll do a good job and will probably agree right away."

"I'll turn her over to you as soon as I get a committee picked, Captain Brackett. We're going to send six volunteers inside the station with her."

"She's a legal prisoner of the police force of this county. You're interfering with the due process of the law."

"Ignore him. Pick your committee."

Mead pointed at the elderly man who had ridden on the platform. "I need some volunteers right away. I'd like you to go inside with her, Mr. Jamison, if you don't mind. You, too, Dr. Sykes. Dr. Salzberg? Please step up here right away if you're willing to help us."

The elderly man stepped forward and the second man Mead pointed at followed him. The third man shook his head and Mead immediately pointed at somebody else.

Brackett raised his mike again. "Nobody is going to mistreat that girl, Dr. Mead. She'll get the same treatment everybody else gets in this county."

"You're making a reasonable request," Nicholson said. "Everybody saw those bruises. You're sending six volunteers in there with her. You want one of them to go with her anywhere she goes."

"I'm making the most reasonable request I can make,

186

Captain Brackett. The girl may have been inciting to riot when you arrested her, but she's showed these people some bruises and she's made some serious accusations, too. I'm sending six volunteers in there with her. We want one of them to go with her anywhere she goes."

"They can go anywhere visitors usually go. They've got the same rights everybody else has."

Nicholson's face hardened. "Don't back down. Tell him there's a limit to what your people can take. You got his prisoner back for him and you're making a reasonable request under the circumstances. Is he trying to provoke a riot, or is he trying to do his job the way the law says he should?"

Heads nodded in the crowd as soon as Mead started talking. Nicholson gave Peggy some more orders and her gang started wandering through the crowd again.

Brackett stepped toward the platform and then paused. He stared at Mead as if he was trying to think.

Nicholson covered his mike with his hand. "This should be just about it. At some point in this situation a riot may help us more than it helps them. The police'll make an intolerable demand and the people on our side will leave the scene feeling like they've been fighting for something reasonable. There's a lot of unknowns in the equation but there's a good chance Hill may decide he can't take the risk."

"You've been playing a hunch all this time," Sue said. "You let Mead do something like that and you didn't even know if it would work."

Brackett looked up at the platform and shrugged. "Tell your people they can come inside with our prisoner, Dr. Mead. They'd better not get in our way but they can come inside. Now hand her over and get out of our way."

Two cops stepped up to the platform. Mead guided the girl down the steps and they grabbed her by the arms. She tossed her head defiantly and they led her toward the courthouse with the six volunteers at their heels.

"Stay right with her," Mead said. "Watch everything they do."

Nicholson took his hand off his mike. "Start signing up volunteers again. Start setting up your patrols for the night."

Sue switched on her mike and gave Peggy's gang an order. Two role players opened up the bin in the bottom of the truck and rolled out the tally counter.

"We're still taking recruits, ladies and gentlemen," Mead said. "Step right up and we'll get our first patrols organized right now. We'll move right out of here and get to work."

People started lining up in front of the counter. Thirty people crowded around Mead and started telling him they thought he'd handled a tough situation better than they'd ever seen anybody handle something like that. A man patted him on the shoulder and told him he was just the kind of man the county needed. Everybody who was signing up at the tally counter was coming back to the platform and joining the crowd around the hero of the hour.

"You can almost see him swelling," Sue said.

"He's getting just the kind of thing he's always wanted," Nicholson said. "He's getting the kind of thing he's always wanted and he'll think we got it for him."

"He would have been in a real mess if you'd been making a wrong guess."

"I was pretty sure I was making the right moves. I couldn't have proved it with the information I had, but the crowd had been acting like they were the kind of people who'd respond to that kind of treatment. I'll have to check it out with the computer tomorrow but it looks to me like we've accomplished something useful even if we never put Boyd out of office. We've got Mead on our side and we've started a political organization that'll be under our control, not Hill's. Mead's going to be a real force around here after tonight. We may not be able to drive Boyd out of office yet, but I don't think they can drive us out of the county, either."

"He would have looked pretty bad if you'd been wrong."

"I doubt if he could have stayed in the county."

Sue shook her head. "I always knew you could be a class-A bastard if you wanted to be."

"It worked," Nicholson said. "I can't claim I can defend it but I'm damned glad I did it now that it's over."

"I'm glad we don't have to do this with the kids watching."

"That's about how I feel."